I0628646

HIGHLAND PROMISE

THE DAUGHTERS OF CLAN DRUMMOND

STEPHANIE MARKS

RED DAGGER

Copyright © 2019 by Stephanie Marks
All rights reserved.
ISBN: 978-0-9940667-8-7

This is a work of fiction. Names, characters, places, and incidents are the product of the author's imagination or are used fictitiously. Any resemblance to actual persons, living or dead, events, or locales is entirely coincidental.

No part of this book may be reproduced in any form or by any electronic or mechanical means, including information storage and retrieval systems, without written permission from the author, except for the use of brief quotations in a book review.

ACKNOWLEDGMENTS

To Ivy. Editor extraordinaire. Thank you for being such an amazing friend.

For D.C.

A NOTE TO MY READERS

I hope that you enjoy this book. If you are interested in finding out about my latest releases, be sure to visit my website to sign up for my newsletter.

- Stephanie

http://www.StephanieMarksBooks.com/

Catriona screamed and dropped her box of painting supplies and the small lantern as she tore herself from his grasp. The flame from the candle went out as the lantern crashed to the ground. They were plunged into darkness. Her attacker lost his balance, and his arms flailed wildly as he tried to right himself on the edge of the top stair. In a desperate attempt to keep himself from tumbling backwards down the tall stair-case, he reached out to catch himself but grasped the front of Catriona's gown as she fled, tearing the front of her bodice almost completely down to her waist.

She ran down the hallway, her heart pounding as if it would leap from her chest, clutching the ragged pieces of her gown together, and tested the door handle of the first bedchamber she came to. Being one of the guest chambers, it was on the first floor of private rooms, and blessedly unlocked.

Relief flooded Catriona's body as she ran through the door and slammed it shut behind her, before barring it quickly to ensure it would keep out her drunken attacker. With a wee bit of luck he might not have seen which door she had escaped through, and it was unlikely that in his current state he would have the fortitude to test them all just to find her.

Shaking, she fell back against the door and tried to catch her breath while she stared down at the tattered pieces of her gown. She clutched at the ruined fabric and tried to suppress the wave of nausea that suddenly overtook her. Just because she was still a maid it did not mean that she was naïve. She knew full well the type of unspeakable misfortune that could happen to a woman when caught unawares by a man whose intentions were less than honorable. She squeezed her eyes shut and tried to block out the terrifying images in her mind of what could have been, but that only made them more vivid.

She opened her eyes with a shuddering breath and forced herself to get ahold of her senses. She had gotten away with little more than a damaged gown and some lost paints, and there was simply no way he would be able to force himself past the barred chamber door. She took another deep breath and her heartbeat began to slow. Everything would be all right. She was safe.

Slowly, she raised her gaze from the floor. Only then did she notice that the room was not unoccupied, as she had first believed it to be. No, there on the bed in front of her, illuminated by the moonlight pouring in from the window, was a very large, very *naked* man.

PROLOGUE

THE HIGHLANDS, Scotland
  Early Spring, 1620

The stars shone brightly in the sky over Lochaber, but that night the moon was little more than a crescent sliver. What little illumination it may have offered was almost completely obscured by wisps of errant clouds, casting the field below into shadow. The lack of moonlight was a small boon to the handful of silent highland men who slipped unseen through the night as they approached a small secluded croft. The seven men crawled on their bellies over to the edge of the low rise, careful to stay downwind from the stable full of horses below. Each man's face was caked with a mixture of mud and soot to obscure his features, but the simple disguise did nothing to conceal the eagerness in each man's eyes.

"Ye each ken yer task, aye? Get those horses rounded up and into the woods." He shivered slightly as a whip of cold air cut across the small ledge he and his men were hidden on. They could not afford to have the cool spring breeze carry their scent to the animals. This moment had been planned too carefully for them to allow a paddock full of spooked horses to be their undoing.

The men lay together in the grass, breathing heavily in anticipation and watched the horse breeder's home carefully for any sign of movement, but all was silent below.

"Have ye the ropes?" His eyes focused on the stable where the horses were kept.

"Aye, Angus" one of his companions whispered back. "We ken what we're about. Let's just do this and get it over with."

"Do ye want to be the one to have to tell him what went wrong if we dinna succeed tonight?"

His impatient companion swallowed audibly and shook his head.

"I did not think so. Now hold yer tongue and wait for my signal. I'll not be forced to go back and tell him why we failed."

The windows in the house had been dark for hours and the cold hard ground had grown uncomfortable beneath them long ago. They had to trust that the horse breeder and his family were fast asleep. It would do them no good to tarry there any longer if they wanted to be well away from the area by sunrise.

"Tis time," said Angus.

The small group of men rushed silently over the hill toward the stable, but one of their number broke away from the group and headed toward the breeder's home.

The renegade member slipped through the darkness, keeping himself low, focused only on his own desires. Propelled forward by a dark need that howled within him.

A firm hand clamped down on his shoulder, halting his departure.

"Where the devil do ye think ye're going?" hissed one of the Scotsmen.

"To take care of the family," the rogue group member told him, placing his hand lightly on the handle of his dirk.

"Ye ken that is not the plan. We're just here to steal the horses. Are ye trying to get us all hanged? Now get yer arse to the stables before the others notice we're gone. If ye draw attention to us I'll slit yer throat for ye, I swear it. Stick to the plan."

The rogue tightened his grip on the handle of his dirk, fighting the roaring urge to plunge it into his partner's chest. He could not stand to be spoken to as though he were a fool, but he would not have to put up with the man for much longer. Soon he would not have to take orders from any of them.

Silently, he jerked his head in a sharp nod, releasing the grip on his knife, and the two men ran towards the stable to help the others steal the horses. He glanced back over his shoulder at the darkened windows of the quiet little house, knowing that soon his needs would be satisfied.

CHAPTER 1

THE HIGHLANDS, Scotland
  Late Spring, 1620

The late spring sun hung low on the distant horizon as Liam and his younger brother Iain led their small group of men down the winding road that would take them to the gates of Drummond Castle. Liam sat up straighter and shifted uncomfortably in his saddle, trying to stretch the tension out of his back without drawing the attention of his men. The trip from Invergarry Castle to the Clan Drummond lands was an easy enough journey over fairly even terrain, but he had pushed his small group of clansmen and their horses to reach the home of Laird Drummond as quickly as possible. It had been three days of hard travel from Lochaber, but they had made good time. And it was time, not comfort, that mattered most.

With a sigh, Liam relaxed back into the saddle as his younger brother Iain drew his horse up alongside him.

Leaning nearer to his elder brother, Iain shot a quick

glance over his shoulder to ensure they would not be overheard by the other men. "Are ye sure Laird Drummond will take the time to speak with us, Liam? I hear tell the man's become a wee bit unhinged in the past year, and that it has made him inhospitable."

"Aye, he'll see us. Inhospitable or no, if the reavers that have been plaguing us are men of his clan, then the man has a duty to see justice done."

Iain eyed him doubtfully. "I dinna suppose ye've bothered to think of a delicate way to broach the subject with him have ye? I still cannot believe ye dinna send the man a letter first, asking to speak with him."

Liam shot his brother a dark look and Iain held a hand up in surrender.

"I'm not saying that this plan of yours is a bit hasty, mind. But ye do have a way about ye that some people, not me of course, but some people may consider a wee bit... terse." The corner of Iain's mouth turned up slightly in a faint smile at his brother's irritated glare.

"I prefer to get to the point of the matter without a lot of frippery, aye. But not all of us were blessed with such a poetic tongue as yours, *brathair*. Maybe ye should put it to better use in politics, instead of seducing all the pretty lasses, if ye are so worried about Laird Drummond taking offense to me. I dinna write to Laird Drummond because I dinna want to give him a chance to say no before I could speak to the man face-to-face. The reavers are attacking us along his border. I want to know that something will be done about it, not receive a prettily worded letter which amounts to little more than kindling for my fire." Deep lines creased Liam's forehead as his mouth turned down in a frown. "I want the man to look me in the eye so that I can judge the truth of what he says. Inhospitable or no, Laird Drummond has a reputation of being an honest and honorable man. I'm sure that given the chance to speak with him, we can get a quick handle on all of this blasted thievery."

Liam tightened the grip on his horse's reins and stared silently off into the distance, focused on the point where Drummond Castle grew larger before them as they made their approach. He took a deep breath and released it slowly. Soon this would all be behind him and he could go back to his life as it should be, without all of these infuriating distractions.

The small group of men rode in silence until they reached Laird Drummond's large courtyard. There was no denying that the castle made for an imposing first impression. The courtyard was flanked by two large buildings. A large plain tower house to the left of the yard and an elegant looking two-level mansion to the right.

He snorted lightly as he eyed the large house. Laird Drummond was one of the wealthiest men in the highlands, and he certainly wasted no opportunity to show it.

The brothers dismounted and handed the reins over to the eager young blonde-haired boy who ran over to meet them. Liam smiled down at the lad and tousled his hair, noticing the distinct streak of dirt across the bridge of the boy's nose. The lad grinned up at him, before leading their two horses away and shouting a friendly greeting to a young man that passed him by. It did not feel so long ago that he and his two younger brothers had been just as covered in grime, laughing and carefree while their mother picked bits of straw out of their hair, caught there from when the boys had been wrestling in the stables.

"Would it be too much of me to ask of ye to try for just a touch of pleasantries?" Iain whispered to him.

Liam narrowed his eyes at his brother then shrugged his shoulders. "I'll be pleasant enough."

7

"I just do not want us ordered out from under his roof before I've had a bath and a bed to sleep in," said Iain.

"With a willing woman to help ye warm the both of them nae doubt."

Iain laughed and slapped his brother on the back.

"Of course. Is there any other way?"

Liam opened his mouth to respond but closed it quickly when one of the Drummond guardsmen came forward to greet them.

"Welcome to Drummond Castle, Laird MacDonell. Laird Drummond has been expecting ye."

"Thank ye," said Liam.

Iain coughed lightly and Liam fought the urge to throttle him. "I've been looking forward to seeing him again," he added.

"If ye'd like to follow me to the great hall while yer men get settled?"

The guard turned toward the entrance of the keep and Liam glared at his brother.

"What?" whispered Iain. "It would not hurt ye to practice yer pleasantries before ye meet Himself, would it?"

"I'll murder ye in yer sleep Iain. Brother or no. I swear to ye I will," Liam grumbled.

He hated to admit it but his brother was right. Laird Drummond's lands were twice the size of his own and the older man was known to enjoy flaunting his wealth. Someone like that expected a certain amount of deference shown him, even from the other clan Chiefs. If Liam wanted the man's help then he was going to have to tread carefully so as to not offend him unduly. Though the thought of having to bow and scrape to the man just to ensure that he dinna accidentally bruise Laird Drummond's ego set Liam's teeth on edge.

The Drummond guard led them into the keep and

through the hallways of the tower house until they came to the large common hall on the first floor.

"If ye did not write to the man," Iain whispered, "then how did he know we were coming?"

Liam did not respond but cast his gaze across the large room, up to the head table where Laird Drummond sat waiting. It was a good question, and one he would be certain to ask the man. Liam did not like the thought of the auld Laird being so privy to Liam's movements.

Their arrival drew the curious glances of the Drummond clansmen sitting at the long tables in the hall, but Liam ignored them, his attention focused on the large man sitting in the centre of the head table.

"Laird MacDonell!" Laird Drummond's voice boomed out as the Chief of Clan Drummond stood to greet them. "Welcome, welcome."

"A bit more hospitable than ye were expecting, then?" Liam whispered to Iain before approaching the older man.

"Aye," his brother whispered back, not taking his eyes off of the chief.

Laird Drummond had been known as a great warrior in his youth. Reckless and wild, his size and strength had been a great asset to him on the battlefield. But after accumulating so much wealth over the years, and after the death of his wife, he had turned his mind to raising his three daughters and had chosen to leave the fighting to younger men. While he was still a formidable man, his great muscles had started to give way to fat. His stomach had softened and he had grown barrel chested, but it was that chest from which his words of welcome were still able to ring out clearly across the hall and reach every corner of the room. And though Laird Drummond may have gotten softer from having spent so much time off the battlefield, Liam could still see the great warrior in him, and why his men would follow him into battle and even to their possible deaths.

"Laird Drummond, thank ye for welcoming me and my men into yer fine home. May I introduce ye to my brother Iain?"

"Iain is it?" The Laird Drummond looked the younger man over. "Ye've grown a bit since the last time I saw ye. Little more than a wee lad then."

"I remember yer visit to Invergarry Castle well, Laird Drummond," Iain said with a graceful bow. "I'm sorry that I've not had a chance to see ye since. I am very pleased to see ye looking so well."

While his brother spouted platitudes, Liam took in the room, casting his gaze about for all possible exits. He turned at the sound of shuffling coming from the doorway behind him and glanced over his shoulder to see the four other clansmen that had come on the journey with him and his brother. They trailed behind one of Laird Drummond's men as they were shown to empty seats at the tables, their weariness from travel clear on their drawn faces.

"Aye Iain, yer right, it's been much too long. You and yer brothers have my condolences on the loss of yer parents. To lose them both like that. It must have been a terrible grief to ye both."

"Thank ye, Laird Drummond," said Liam, his voice solemn. "My father always spoke very highly of ye and counted ye as a friend. He always said ye were a good man."

"High praise indeed, coming from a man as honorable as yer father." Laird Drummond lowered his gaze to the table before him for a short moment before clapping his hands together and waving Iain and Liam forward.

"Enough of these solemn matters. The two of ye are here now, and new friendships are to be made." He let out a booming laugh as Liam and Iain climbed the steps to the dais and waved them toward the two empty chairs to Laird Drummond's right.

On his left hand side two of three seats were occupied by two beautiful young women who looked to be near Liam and Iain in age. The older-looking one held herself with an air of dignity wrapped around her that she wore like a mantle. Her deep, rich brown hair was plaited in a single thick braid over one shoulder that reached down to her slender waist. Her features were striking, but she had an air about her that made Liam feel as though any man would be taking his life into his hands if he was to approach her with anything resembling romance on his mind. She was gorgeous and yet completely untouchable. Like a beautiful, poisonous flower.

The younger daughter leaned casually in her chair, laughing as she spoke to her sister and absentmindedly catching a wayward strand of deep auburn hair that had escaped from her ribbon, and brushing it away from her face. Unlike the older sister, she appeared to be much more relaxed. He watched as she took a long drink out of her glass before she continued happily chatting away. Liam knew that there was a third daughter, but she was nowhere to be seen.

"These are my daughters. Lady Aileen, my eldest, and Lady Bridget. I have to make my apologies for my youngest. She will not be joining us for supper."

The two young women barely glanced up to look at them, but nodded politely before quickly returning to their hushed conversation. Even though it happened quickly, Liam did not miss the looks of irritation on both of the young ladies' faces. He was not sure if the young women were irritated by the absence of their younger sibling or by the presence of Liam and his. Either way, they did not spare he and Iain another glance.

Liam was fine with that. He would rather be ignored than

11

fawned over by a couple of foolish young lasses with nary a thought in their heads for anything but gossip and fripperies.

Wine and food were quickly brought over to them but Liam could not relax enough to truly enjoy it. After three days in the saddle, he was eager to get down to the business at hand, but Laird Drummond insisted on regaling him with stories of the older man's youth. Liam made as much idle talk as he could before he thought he would be driven mad with boredom.

"Laird Drummond," he interjected when it looked as if the other man was preparing to launch into another long story. "The reason we have traveled all this way is because I need to speak with you about a matter of grave importance."

"Aye, and what's that then?" Laird Drummond asked as he impaled a piece of meat on the end of his knife.

Liam reminded himself that he must tread carefully. As welcoming as the man had been up until then, he would not take kindly to accusations.

"Reports have made their way to me about reaving on my land. All manner of livestock have been going missing over the past few weeks…" Liam paused and considered how best to continue. "The thefts have all taken place along the border of our lands. Have you by any chance heard similar reports of reaving on yer land as well?"

Liam watched the older man carefully for any sign of reaction to his words, but Laird Drummond did not so much as blink.

"Reavers? Nay, I've not heard reports of any. But I don't see why ye'd come all this way for a bit of pilfering."

Liam shook his head. "If it were just a bit of pilfering then I wouldn't have bothered. But I'm not talking about a wee *creach*. This is robbery pure and simple."

Laird Drummond chewed carefully as he considered Liam's words.

"Ye're a small clan, MacDonell. Perhaps someone is testing ye."

Liam frowned at the man's words. The MacDonell clan was not so small as all that. His lands were simply not as vast as those belonging to Laird Drummond. But where The MacDonell's lacked land they made up for it in the wealth of their resources. The fields were extremely fertile and yielded the heartiest of crops year in and year out. And their livestock was known as some of the best in the highlands. People came from all over Scotland to barter for their prize horses.

"If it's a fight someone's after, then it's one they'll get," Liam said firmly.

Something flashed in Laird Drummond's eyes, but he simply smiled and raised his glass to Liam.

"I have nae doubt, my boy. Yer father was always a fighter. Something I'm sure ye've inherited from him. But there's something to be said for having the support of yer friends, now, isn't there?"

Liam was puzzled, unsure of what the man was getting at. He glanced over at his brother, but Iain was busy flirting with one of their serving maids, paying no mind to the conversation Liam was having with their host.

"I'm not sure I understand yer meaning, Laird Drummond."

"I'm sure yer troubles are no more than a temporary situation, but if it turns out that they're not, and someone is setting up to make a move against ye, I've nae doubt that ye'd be grateful for the help my clan could provide ye…"

"It would be very much appreciated, aye," said Liam hesitantly, unsure of where the auld Laird was leading the conversation.

"Well, then. The only thing for it is for ye to wed one of my daughters."

Liam froze, not certain if he had heard the man correctly.

"Ye want me to wed one of yer daughters?" he asked slowly. Out of the corner of his eye he saw Iain spin toward him, the serving girl instantly forgotten.

"Aye." Laird Drummond lifted his cup and took a long sip of wine. "There be nothing like a marriage to strengthen an alliance."

Liam's gaze slid over to the two young women sitting next to his father. They were not looking in his direction, but Liam could tell by the rigid set of their shoulders that they had heard their father's suggestion. The red-head turned and shot a look of horror at her father before sliding and icy glance in Liam's direction.

They were bonnie lasses the both of them, but at eight and twenty Liam had already been married once and had sworn off doing it for a second time. He sat silently a moment, weighing his words carefully, unsure of how to turn down the offer without having a second potential battle on his hands.

"I thank ye for yer offer, Laird Drummond. It is a generous one indeed. But unfortunately, it is one that I will have to turn down, as I will never marry."

The smile slipped from Laird Drummond's face, and he lowered his cup of wine. Liam could tell that he had offended the man by refusing the offer, but he simply could not wed one of his daughters. Especially when they were so obviously against the idea. Liam had never been one to force himself on a woman. He didn't relish the idea of spending the rest of his life with a wife who wanted nothing to do with him. He'd already had some experience of what that was like and was determined to not repeat the experience.

"Are ye refusing my offer of marriage? Are they not bonny enough for ye? Do ye think ye're above marrying my precious girls?" The Laird's voice rose with every word, drawing the attention of everyone in the room.

"Laird Drummond, I meant no offense to ye or your daughters, sir, I simply... cannot. I have no intentions to marry, now or in the future. If marriage is the price of your help, then the cost ye demand of me is too high, and I have no choice but to seek help elsewhere. I think it might be best if my men and I were on our way." Liam pushed back his chair and made to rise from his seat, but his movement was halted by Laird Drummond's hand on his arm.

"Nay. Ye've had a long ride. I'll not have it said that my pride drove ye from my table. Spend the night under my roof. Tomorrow ye can be on yer way."

Laird Drummond waved over a young servant girl and indicated toward Liam and Iain.

"Show Laird MacDonell and his brother to their rooms, lass. They'll be spending the night."

Liam and Iain rose from their chairs and bowed stiffly to Laird Drummond and his daughters before following the servant out of the hall.

"Well," said Iain thoughtfully. "At least he dinna demand we leave."

"Aye well," Liam sighed, "there's still time."

CHAPTER 2

THE STABLE WAS dark and silent except for the sound of sleeping horses. A squat tallow candle burned in its lantern, casting a low light in the stall. It did nothing to ward off the cool night air as Catriona hurried to unsaddle and brush down her horse as quickly and quietly as she could. She tiptoed around the stall, careful to avoid bumping the lantern from its hook while trying to not disturb the other horses in the stable. The last thing she needed was to alert any passing guard to her presence.

A faint shuffling came from above her and Catriona froze. She squeezed her eyes shut and sent up a silent prayer, her fingers clutched tightly to the horse brush in her hands. She had made it this far without discovery, God could not possibly be so cruel as to let her get caught now. She crept out of the stall and looked up at the ledges above her, trying to see who was there, but all she could make out were the shadowy edges of piles of hay.

"Hello?" she whispered quietly, but blessedly, there was no reply.

One of the young stable lads must have fallen asleep in

the hay loft. Suddenly, there was more shuffling and a slender arm slipped down over the side of the ledge. She held her breath and waited to see if the boy awoke, but he did not move again. Catriona sighed with relief and grabbed the lantern off of its hook. Careful to not disturb the sleeping stable lad, she slipped silently out of the stable and closed the door firmly behind her.

She had stayed out for far too long, and if her father found out about her sneaking back home at such a late hour, he would blister her ears for her and most likely ban her from leaving the keep as well. She had not meant to stay out for so long. She had fallen asleep in the clearing, and when she awoke the moon had been high in the sky. Time always escaped her when she was painting. It was not as though she defied her father on purpose, but when she had a brush in her hand, the world simply fell away and time held no meaning. Unfortunately, no amount of explaining that to her father would save her from whatever punishment he saw fit to bestow upon her. Her elder sisters accused her of being their father's favorite, and insisted that he went easier on her than he did on them, but sometimes she felt as though he punished her extra in an attempt to prove them wrong. Tonight was certainly not the night she wanted to put their accusations to the test.

Catriona was cold, hungry, and desperately wanted a bath. She was sore from sleeping on the ground and irritated with herself for missing supper, but she supposed that's what she got for only packing a light lunch with her that morning.

She hurried across the courtyard and up to the main doors of the mansion. As she made her way inside she considered what her chances were of getting caught if she tried to sneak into the kitchen to find something to eat. The promise of cheese and roasted meat called to her but it simply was not worth the risk. She would just have to ignore the rumbling of her stomach and wait until breakfast.

Catriona hurried through the hallways with her small box of paints and brushes clutched close to her chest, and her lantern held high. She made for the staircase, trying to ignore the pangs of hunger as her stomach growled in protest, when an unexpected shadow crossed her path.

"What's this, now?" A low, rough voice came out of the darkness.

She stifled a scream as a tall man stumbled out of the darkness in front of her. He pressed one hand against the wall to hold himself upright, and Catriona could make out a large, pale-brown stain down the front of his shirt. "What's such a bonny lass doing out of bed at this hour? Snuck off to see your sweetheart did ye?" he slurred.

The distinct smell of whiskey mingled with the sour odor of vomit assaulted her nose as he shuffled slowly towards her while continuing to lean heavily against the wall.

Catriona clutched her box of painting supplies more closely to her chest and adjusted the lantern so that she could better make out the man's face. It was still too well hidden with the distance between them being too great from where she was standing.

Her heart pounded and her palms grew damp as a little voice in the back of her head told her to run. She had never been afraid in her own home before. While she could scare conceive of the idea, every part of her being told her that she should flee.

"Do not take one step closer," she told him as firmly as possible. She had tried to sound commanding, but even she was unconvinced. She could hear the wavering from uncertainty and fear in her own voice, and she did not doubt that he had heard it as well.

The man took a shuffling step forward out of the shadows, at last allowing Catriona to make out his features in the dim light. She studied his face intently, but she was certain that she had never seen him before. He was not one of her father's men, nor anyone that she could remember having visited the castle before in the past. She did not recognize him at all, so what was he doing inside the manor, and in such a drunken state? Why was he not in the keep? Only the family and her father's most honored guests were offered a room in the manor, and if this man was an honored guest then she would eat her paint brushes.

"Come 'ere, lass, 'n givvus a kiss, then. Thassa toll ye must pay me if ye want up these stairs."

"I'll not be kissing ye this night or any other. Now, I demand ye let me pass at once." Emboldened by her ire at his inconceivable demands Catriona squared her shoulders and proceeded forward. She prayed that if she appeared to be unafraid he would lose interest and allow her to pass. Everyone was sure to have gone to bed long ago, so even if she tried to call for help it was unlikely anyone would hear her. Especially as there were no bedchambers on this floor.

Her heart raced as each step she took brought her closer to the drunken stranger. Her eyes stayed fixed on his as she proceeded to step past him, trying to anticipate his movements.

His narrow eyes watched her just as closely as she came near, peering at her intently from the shallow sockets in his long narrow face. A week's worth of unkept beard grew unevenly along his jaw and down his neck, and the errant thought that the man was in need of a shave was passing through her mind when his hand suddenly lashed out to grab her.

"Just one quick kiss," the man said, and lunged for her.

With a shriek, Catriona sidestepped him and broke out into a run. She dashed past the drunk man and made for the staircase as quickly as possible. It would be far safer on the upper floors than rushing back out into the darkness of night.

"Hold on, now," the man said, chasing her up the staircase. "Yer not going to get away that easy."

Catriona could hear his uneven footsteps behind her and heavy thumping, as though he were falling against the wall as he climbed, but she did not turn around to see. All that mattered was putting as much distance between the two of them as possible.

But she had not moved fast enough. As Catriona reached the top of the stairs, he grabbed her arm. He tugged her backwards. The unexpected force caused her to stumble, and he spun her to face him.

Catriona screamed and dropped her box of painting supplies and the small lantern as she tore herself from his grasp. The flame from the candle went out as the lantern crashed to the ground. They were plunged into darkness. Her attacker lost his balance, and his arms flailed wildly as he tried to right himself on the edge of the top stair. In a desperate attempt to keep himself from tumbling backwards down the tall staircase, he reached out to catch himself but grasped the front of Catriona's gown as she fled, tearing the front of her bodice almost completely down to her waist.

She ran down the hallway, her heart pounding as if it would leap from her chest, clutching the ragged pieces of her gown together, and tested the door handle of the first bedchamber she came to. Being one of the guest chambers, it was on the first floor of private rooms, and blessedly unlocked.

Relief flooded Catriona's body as she ran through the door and slammed it shut behind her, before barring it quickly to ensure it would keep out her drunken attacker. With a wee bit of luck he might not have seen which door she had escaped through, and it was unlikely that in his current state he would have the fortitude to test them all just to find her.

Shaking, she fell back against the door and tried to catch her breath while she stared down at the tattered pieces of her gown. She clutched at the ruined fabric and tried to suppress the wave of nausea that suddenly overtook her. Just because she was still a maid it did not mean that she was naïve. She knew full well the type of unspeakable misfortune that could happen to a woman when caught unawares by a man whose intentions were less than honorable. She squeezed her eyes shut and tried to block out the terrifying images in her mind of what could have been, but that only made them more vivid.

She opened her eyes with a shuddering breath and forced herself to get ahold of her senses. She had gotten away with little more than a damaged gown and some lost paints, and there was simply no way he would be able to force himself past the barred chamber door. She took another deep breath and her heartbeat began to slow. Everything would be all right. She was safe.

Slowly, she raised her gaze from the floor. Only then did she notice that the room was not unoccupied, as she had first believed it to be. No, there on the bed in front of her, illuminated by the moonlight pouring in from the window, was a very large, very *naked* man.

CHAPTER 3

LIAM WOKE WITH A START, torn from a deep, dreamless slumber. He lurched up in bed as the echoes of a loud slamming door rang in his ears. Reaching for the *sgian dubh* he had hidden beneath his pillow before he had gone to sleep, his eyes scanned the room for danger. But even as his hand wrapped around the cool slender hilt of the short knife, he found himself staring into the astounded heart-shaped face of a beautiful young woman.

"What are ye doing in my bedchamber?"

Perhaps his brother had found a willing serving lass to entertain him for the night. If so, he was not in the mood for such games. All he wanted was to go back to sleep so that they could get out from under Laird Drummond's roof and back on the road as early as possible.

"I..." she began in a whisper, but her soft voice trailed off. Her wide eyes darted around the chamber, landing everywhere but on him, and in the low light he was able to see the color rise in her cheeks.

It took him a moment to remember that he had gone to sleep in naught but his skin. The chamber had been stifling hot even though it was only late spring and he had chosen to sleep atop the bed clothes in an attempt to keep cool.

Liam moved quickly and released the blade he held, grabbing the pillow instead and placed it upon his bare lap. If his nakedness was the cause of her obvious discomfort, then it was unlikely she had found her way to his room with the intent to bed him, but what other reason could there be for her to come to his chamber at such a late hour?

"Ye did not answer my question, lass. Did my brother send ye to me?"

"I'm sorry. I'm so sorry. I did not know anyone would be in here. Please forgive my intrusion. I'll take my leave immediately."

The apology came tumbling out of the young lass in a rush of words. She spun around to face the door, and stumbled slightly, tripping over her skirts in her haste. But once her back was fully turned to him she suddenly hesitated, her hand frozen as she reached out to take hold of the bar across the door.

She looked back at him questioningly over her shoulder and to the door again, her mouth turned down in a frown, and deep lines creased her forehead as she bit her bottom lip.

Even from across the room, the moon illuminated her face enough for Liam to see the shimmer of unshed tears beginning to gather in the girl's eyes. She closed her eyes and took a shaky breath as though trying to convince herself not to cry, and that's when he noticed that she kept her hands up to her breast because she was trying to hold the torn pieces of her gown together.

"Are ye well? Has something happened to ye?" He reached slowly for his shirt, which he had placed on the chair next to his bed, while trying to keep himself covered.

"There was a man in the hallway. He attacked me—" Her voice cracked and Liam's heart tugged at the sound. He wanted to go to her and comfort her somehow. But he doubted the girl would find much comfort in a man wearing only his shirt after what had just happened to her.

Would that he had his brother's gifted tongue. Iain would have known what to say to her to calm her and ease her fear.

"Did he hurt ye? Force himself on ye, I mean?" He coughed, and looked around the room before his eyes were drawn back to her. This was not the kind of conversation he was used to having with a young women that he did not know, or one that he did know, for that matter.

She shook her head and squared her shoulders, looking not away from him in shame, but meeting his gaze squarely. "No, I was able to get away. He tore my gown, no more than that. Though I'm afraid he might still be out there looking for me. I'm very sorry for the intrusion."

The color flushed more darkly in her cheeks, and she held herself tightly.

Liam couldn't help but be impressed with the young woman. Though obvious in her embarrassment about their state of undress, she clearly refused to be cowed by the events of the night. Most women would have been in hysterics had a strange man tried to force himself on them, but this lass seemed determined to keep her wits about her.

He could not remember the last time he had spoken with such a practical woman, especially one as beautiful as she was. Those he had met that were as fair of face usually had naught but sea foam between their ears.

Liam took in the way her honey-gold hair framed her face, and the gentle curves of her body beneath her ruined gown. He shifted uncomfortably, suddenly feeling himself growing harder. He had not been with a woman in over a month, but his reaction to this young woman made him feel guilty. What kind of a man lusted after a lass that was in such obvious distress? While he may not have his brother's charms, Liam was not a complete brute either. Although it would be near-impossible to convince her of that fact if he continued to stand there in naught but his shirt, as it would soon betray his ever-increasing condition.

"Would ye mind turning 'round a moment?" he asked her. "If ye let me get dressed I can go out and see if he is still there." And the sooner he was able to get dressed the less likely he would embarrass the both of them with the chance of her catching sight of the state of him.

"Oh, thank—"

"WHERE IS SHE?"

The young woman's expression of gratitude was cut short by Laird Drummond's booming voice echoing down the hallway.

As Liam reached for his plaid, a heavy pounding thudded at the door.

"Open the door MacDonell, I know she's in there. I demand ye open the door this instant before I kick it down. If ye've hurt her I swear I'll send yer sorry soul straight to the devil!"

Liam cringed, his arm outstretched towards his plaid, but as the pounding continued against the door of his bedchamber he realized that he had no time to finish getting dressed.

He crossed the room in a few long strides and placed a hand lightly on the young woman's shoulder, maneuvering her out of the way. As he unbarred the door he saw that what little color she had left had drained from his late-night visitor's face, and a feeling of dread settled over him.

He had already offended Laird Drummond once that night. What new problems had this young woman brought with her?

Liam unbarred the door, and started to open it, but the moment Laird Drummond saw his chance he shoved through it, knocking Liam back and out of his way. Even though Liam stood a few inches taller than the man, Laird Drummond was able to force himself into the room, strengthened by the depth of his fury.

The Laird took one look at Liam wearing nothing but his shirt, and the torn gown on the young woman in his room and whirled on Liam in a thundering rage.

"How dare ye MacDonell! Is this how ye think to repay my hospitality?"

"Laid Drummond, please, I can explain."

"Oh, aye, ye'll explain. Explain to me how ye could reject my offer to wed one of my daughters to ye, and then go and have yer way with my youngest!"

The blood ran cold in Liam's veins as his mind tried frantically to make sense of the words he was hearing. His youngest daughter? It could not be. God would not be so cruel as to play a game with him such as this.

"No, Da!" the lass protested, but Liam hardly heard her.

"I never touched her!" Liam shouted, outraged that the man would think to suggest he would be capable of such a thing.

"Ye'd lie right to my face and dishonor my family under my own roof?" Laid Drummond seethed. "She was seen going into yer room. I have a witness! And now here I find her, with her gown torn while ye stand there as good as naked!"

"I did not touch her!" Liam shouted. "I demand that ye produce this witness. Then they can tell ye the truth of the matter. That the lass's gown was already ripped long before she entered here."

Catriona gasped and Liam saw that the color had flowed back into her cheeks, far from pale, they were now a deep flaming red.

He winced, sorry for the carelessness of his words. He

had not meant to humiliate her any more than she already was, but he refused to be accused of her ruin.

Their raised voices had drawn a small crowd and now the hallway outside of his bedchamber was full of people, witnesses to Laird Drummond's accusations. It would not be long before word spread throughout the highlands that Laird Liam MacDonell had disgraced Laird Drummond's youngest daughter.

"Ye've shamed the girl, MacDonell and I demand that ye do right by her. The two of ye will be wed on the morrow."

Laird Drummond grabbed his daughter by the arm and pulled her roughly from Liam's bedchamber, slamming the door behind them.

Liam stood alone in the darkness, and the sudden silence in the room was almost deafening. He felt as though he had just been trampled by an entire herd of horses. Laird Drummond had made his accusations before witnesses, and demanded that Liam righted his supposed wrong. There was nothing that Liam could do. Honor dictated that he must marry the girl unless he wanted to leave her shamed.

Seconds rolled by as his mind scrambled for a solution. There had to be a way out of this. Wed? He could not be wed! The very idea was beyond unthinkable. But no answer came, and he was suddenly overcome with exhaustion. His mind continued to reel as he climbed onto the bed and lay on his back, staring up at the cracks in the stones in the ceiling. He lay there, waiting for sleep to reclaim him and followed the lines in the stone and the patterns that they formed. It was only after some time had passed that it struck him, the pattern of his own night that he had been too caught off guard to see. Laird Drummond had achieved exactly what he had wanted. Liam would be marrying one of Drummond's daughters after all.

Liam sat up, and grabbed the nearest thing to him, an

earthen jug of water, and hurled it against the wall, where it smashed into pieces, leaving water splashed down the wall and over the floor.

His hands curled into fists as the fury rose within him. Laird Drummond and his angelic-faced daughter had played him for a fool.

"Da, please! Ye must listen to me!" Catriona begged as she hurried to try to keep up with her father's determined strides. She tripped over the sagging hem of her gown as he pulled her down the hallway toward the bedchambers where she and her sisters slept, and struggled to stay on her feet rather than flat on her face in the middle of the hallway. Her father tugged on her arm and she winced in pain at his tight grip.

"I'll not hear another word about it, Catriona. The man has shamed ye and our family, and now I'll be making sure he does right by ye. Ye'll be married to The MacDonell tomorrow afternoon, and that's my final word on it."

"But he did not touch me, I swear to ye! He did not lay a hand on me. There was another," she tried to frantically to explain. "A drunk man in the hallway. He was not known to me, I had never set eyes on him before in my life, I am sure of it. He lunged at me and tore my dress, but no more. I was able to get away before he was able to harm me further, and it was to Laird MacDonell's chamber I fled, though I didn't know it to be occupied at the time." Her father said nothing as he stormed down the hall toward her bedchamber.

"Da, do ye understand? Why will ye not listen to me? I'm telling ye that I was attacked by someone else. This has all been a terrible mistake. Da, please! Do not make me do this. Do not make me marry the man. I dinna even know him, nor him me. This is not fair, Da, ye cannot blame him for the fault of another!"

Laird Drummond turned sharply on his daughter and Catriona let out a short shriek as she stumbled, almost colliding with her father's chest. He grabbed her tightly by the shoulders and backed her up against the wall, then pointed a long finger towards her face. She winced at the pain of his blunt fingertips digging into her skin but she dared not speak. She had never before seen her father so angry, and while he had always shown great affection for all three of his daughters, he had always doted on her a little more than her elder sisters.

"Listen to me, lass, because I am only going to tell ye this once, understand?" His voice was low and menacing and Catriona nodded quickly, blinking back the unshed tears which burned in her eyes. "Ye were found alone in his room with the pair of ye in a state of undress. It does not matter if he touched ye or not, the damage is done. 'Tis my own fault I suppose. I've let ye and yer sisters run wild through this castle for too long. Was my own selfishness, 'tis true. I love having ye and yer sisters near to me. But it's time ye were wed, lass, and The MacDonell is a wealthy man. Ye'll be well taken care of. So I'll not have ye ruining this opportunity. Is that understood?"

Catriona could do nothing but nod as her mind raced. Did her father not care at all that a man had tried to attack her? Would he just let him go free?

"And the other man? Are ye going to look for the other man?" she whispered. "The one that truly attacked me?"

"Hear me well, for I'll only be saying it once. There was no other man."

Tears streamed silently down Catriona's face as she let her father rush her the rest of the way to her bedchamber.

CHAPTER 4

CATRIONA STOOD at the large window of her bedchamber and gazed out across the broad expanse of gardens below. It was a beautiful spring day, with the bright shining sun a rare and welcome sight in the pale blue sky. A chorus of birds trilled outside her window, and her heart ached at their hopeful chirps. She longed for their sense of freedom. How sweet it would be to spread her wings and take flight. In a few short wingbeats, she would be far gone from here, forever free from what awaited her. She closed her eyes tilted her face up toward the sky, letting the sunshine warm her skin. She fought back the tears that threatened to fall.

It was the perfect day. It was the kind of day she would very much have wished to be married on. Married to a man she loved and who loved her with his whole heart. But now that would never be.

She turned from the window and stood in front of her two elder sisters, dressed in her finest gown. Her fingers nervously pleated the soft sky-blue fabric of the full skirt while she chewed on her bottom lip and wished the birds chirping away happily outside her window to the deepest pits of Hades.

"I cannot do this," she gasped. Her stomach was tangled in knots, and she was suddenly finding it harder and harder to breathe.

"Ye dinna have a choice, Cat," said Aileen. Her eldest sister circled her slowly and adjusted one of the flowers tucked into the intricate arrangement of tiny plaits pinned up in Catriona's hair.

"But I do not even know him. How can da expect me to marry someone that I do not even know?" Catriona wailed.

"Stop it, Cat," Aileen said tersely. "Ye knew this day would eventually come. And ye brought it on yerself by running around at all hours of the night. What were ye thinking coming back so late?"

"Oh, leave her alone, Aileen!" said Brigid. She got up from the bed and took Catriona's hand in her own, squeezing it reassuringly. "It is not as though Cat asked Laird MacDonell to ravish her. The man is obviously a brute. Can ye not see how scared our sister is? She's as white as milk, and her hands are ice cold. How would ye like to be forced to wed a man that had shamed ye so?"

Aileen scowled at Brigid but did not respond, continuing to fuss over Catriona's gown and hair instead.

Catriona opened her mouth but wavered. Da had forbade her from mentioning the happenings of the night before to anyone. Catriona and her sisters had never had secrets among themselves. They were not only sisters but best friends, and after today when would she see them again? She hated the idea of leaving them like this, especially with them believing a lie, and the worst about her. How could she possibly go off to start a life with a man she did not know under a cloud of scandal and shame? While there may be nothing she could do to quell the gossip among the rest of the clansmen, she did not have to live with her sisters believing the story their father was forcing her to tell.

"He dinna ravish me," she whispered.

Aileen's hands froze in Catriona's hair, and Brigid eyed her shrewdly.

"What do ye mean, Cat?" Brigid asked.

"Laird MacDonell never laid a finger on me." She lowered her gaze to the floor, unable to meet their eyes. Just saying the words out loud filled her with shame. She was not the only one who would have to live with the scandal of people believing he was less than honorable.

"He was a complete gentleman. I was attacked by a man in the hallway and ran into the nearest bedchamber to escape. I thought it would be empty, but Laird MacDonell was inside. He was just about to go out into the hall to ensure it was safe for me to make my way back to my chamber when Da showed up and demanded we be wed."

"Do ye know the man who attacked ye?" Brigid asked.

"No, he was not familiar to me."

"Maybe he was one of MacDonell's men?" said Aileen.

"I dinna know. But he reeked of spirits." Catriona clutched at the skirt of her gown. "I told Da what happened, but…" She trailed off. What could explain Da's strange reaction to what happened to her?

"But what?" Aileen encouraged her.

"He dinna care. He said that The MacDonell was a rich man, and that I was not to speak about what happened and ruin this opportunity." She shook her head. How could her da have demanded such a thing of her? "I was such a fool! I never should have lingered so long in Laird MacDonell's chamber. I was just so scared, and now the man is being forced to marry me. I've ruined both his life and mine, and all because I fell asleep painting like a wee fool! He must hate me. This is all my fault!" Catriona burst into tears.

Her sisters hugged her tightly as she cried, whispering soothing words of encouragement. But it did no good.

"Aileen, ye dinna think?" asked Brigid as she wiped the tears from Catriona's face.

"Dinna be ridiculous, Brigid," Aileen said, hushing her.

"What is it?" asked Catriona.

"Nothing," said Brigid with a weak smile. "Pay no mind."

A look passed between her sisters that Catriona did not understand, but she was too weary to think on it for long.

There was a knock at the door, and a moment later their father entered in his finery. The buttons on his coat were polished to a high shine, and a triumphant smile graced his freshly shaven face.

"Ye're an absolute vision lass. I've never seen a lovelier bride." Laird Drummond swept his youngest daughter up into a tight hug that lifted her clear off her feet, and kissed her on the cheek before putting her back down again.

"Aye, just look at her happy face," Brigid muttered snidely under her breath.

"What was that, Brigid?" Laird Drummond asked, frowning at his middle daughter.

"I said, 'Aye, what a happy day,' Da," said Brigid loudly with forced cheer.

"Aye, aye, a happy day indeed. The first of my wee bairns to leave me. And the two of ye will be next. Make no mistake. I ken it might not seem fair now, what with little Cat being the youngest. But I promise ye both that I'll make fine matches for ye before long. Just ye both wait and see. Fine, fine matches." He laughed and clapped his hands together. "Come now. We mustn't keep the minister waiting."

Laird Drummond swept from the room in high spirits and did not see the looks of confusion and fear that passed between his three daughters behind his back.

Catriona watched the retreating figure of her father and

blinked back a fresh torrent of tears. How casually her father dismissed his betrayal of his youngest daughter. After unclenching her hands, Catriona gazed down at the red crescent moons embedded in her palms, left there from the sharp edges of her fingernails.

"Come along, Cat," Aileen whispered, clasping one of Catriona's sore hands in her own. "There's nothing to be done about it now. Father will not stop this wedding, so you had best not keep Laird MacDonell waiting."

Catriona wanted to tell Aileen that The MacDonell could wait for her in hell for all she cared, but she was not as bold as her sister Brigid. So instead, she nodded her head sharply and took her first step towards an unknown future.

Liam paced back and forth in the small kirk while he waited for the arrival of his bride. *Bride*. He cringed at the word, and cursed the entire farce of a wedding.

"Are ye going to just stand there and do nothing, or are ye going to help me find a way to get out of this?" he snapped at Iain.

The priest looked over at the sound of Liam's raised voice and gave him a disapproving glare. Liam ignored the priest and continued pacing. The sound of his boots on the stone floor echoed around the room as he stormed back and forth, his hands clenched in tight fists at his side.

Iain crossed his arms over his chest and leaned against one of the front pews.

"I dinna ken what ye expect me to do *brathair*. Laird Drummond accused ye of shaming his daughter in front of God the Almighty and a hallway full of witnesses. And ye said yourself that ye were standing there in naught but yer shirt. What was the man to think?"

"Have ye not listened to a word I've said? He did not discover me with his daughter. I am telling ye Iain, the whole thing was a plot. Can ye not see that this is all too convenient? Last night I turned down his offer of marriage, and today I'm to wed his youngest. Ye cannot be so naïve as to think this is merely coincidence. It is obviously some scheme that he and his angelic-faced viper of a daughter concocted in order to entrap me."

"Do ye really think that he and the lass came up with something as elaborate as all of that, just to get ye to the altar? Laird Drummond is one of the wealthiest Chiefs in the area. Why would he be so desperate to have his lass be wed to ye? I'm sorry, Liam, but I see no treachery here. Just a bit of bad luck."

"'A bit of bad luck?'" Liam's face was thunderous, and he gave serious consideration to throttling his brother right there in the house of God. "Ye think 'tis just a bit of bad luck that I am going to be trapped in a second loveless marriage to a scheming liar? No matter how angelic of face, the lass has proven herself to be an opportunistic little wretch. And I'll be damned if you or they or anyone in this blasted village think that I'm going to marry her today or ever. I'd rather die, Iain, than be forced to marry another woman like that."

Iain's expression softened and he placed a comforting hand on his brother's shoulder. "The lass is not Fiona, Liam. Ye cannot damn her without knowing the truth of it."

"The simple fact that I find myself in this position is all the proof I need. And to think I wanted to protect her from her mystery assailant." He snorted mirthlessly and jabbed a finger in his brother's direction. "She must think me a fool to have conned me so easily! But they cannot force me to go through with it. I will not go through with it!" he shouted. Anger and regret swirled within him, and he fought back a wave of nausea. "I cannot get married again, Iain," Liam whispered.

"And if ye're wrong? Would ye leave the lass shamed then, Liam? Her reputation is destroyed whether ye meant to do it or not. Her name will always be tied to yours. And if ye run and abandon her now, ye'll lose the respect of yer clan. Ye must do this Liam. I'm sorry, but ye must."

The doors to the kirk opened, and the guests streamed in to fill the pews. It had only been half a day, but news traveled fast when Laird Drummond set about securing a kirk and a priest to wed his youngest daughter. Those that had heard news of the scandal were eager to see it play out to the end.

Liam's own men were among the crowd, each one looking distinctly uncomfortable. What would they think of their Chief if he were to simply walk out of those doors and not return? How would he explain to them the truth of what happened, and expose Laird Drummond and his daughter for the liars that they were? No, it was a fine dream, but not one that would ever come to pass.

Damn him, Iain was right. There was no help for it, he would have to marry the Drummond girl. The cost of walking out those doors was too great. And even if he did try to leave, there was a likely chance that Drummond would simply order his men to cut Liam down where he stood.

Once everyone was seated, Laird Drummond's two elder daughters entered. They both wore matching expressions of distrust on their faces as they looked upon Liam before taking their seats in one of the front pews.

Liam wiped his damp palms across his plaid. There was no escaping it now. He was surrounded with no place to run, and even if he could escape, he could not spend the rest of his life knowing that his people believed he had ruined a young innocent lass.

The doors opened for a second time, and Liam swallowed

the lump in his throat when Laird Drummond entered with Catriona on his arm. The lass was a vision. The long pale blonde strands of her hair had been plaited and pinned up around her head in an elaborate way, but a few tendrils had been left loose to frame her soft face. He had thought that her eyes had been wide last night due to her fear, but today he saw that they were truly as big as Loch Eil, and a clear crystal blue, deep enough to drown in.

She was a true beauty, and now he remembered the way his body had reacted to her the night before. He searched her face for something, anything that would convince him that he was wrong about her. He wanted to believe Iain when he said that she was most likely innocent of any scheme. He searched for any sign that would give him a glimmer of hope to ease the tempest of rage and suspicion swirling within him, but there was none. As she walked down the aisle toward him, there was nothing of the sweet, innocent lass from the night before. No determination and strength in her eyes. Her face betrayed no emotion at all, and her blue eyes were cold, hard and empty. Just as Fiona's had been.

Liam clenched his jaw and silently cursed both her and her father as she took her place beside him and prepared to say the words that would forever bind them in the eyes of God and man.

CHAPTER 5

CATRIONA SAT, maudlin, at the head table and tried in vain to ignore the mob of guests that filled the great hall. It looked as though the entire village had come to wish her and her new husband well in their blessed union. So many had come to celebrate her joyous day—or revel in the scandal of her great shame. However one chose to look at it. It was amazing that so many people had been able to make their way to the castle for her wedding dinner with less than a single day's notice. Who would have thought that news of her humiliating situation would have proven to be such a great motivator? Though she would have preferred not to think of it at all, which was why she was already on her fifth glass of wine and the sun had yet to set. She had never had much of a taste for drink. She had also never felt such a powerful desire to let her senses slip from her grasp, to turn her back on the harsh reality that was her life.

Apart from her wedding vows she had not said two words to her new husband. She hadn't dared. Every time she glanced his way she saw naught but fury in his eyes. His obvious disgust and hatred of her cut her to the marrow. He had seemed kind the night before, even gentle once he had gotten over his initial surprise at her unexpected arrival, but any concern he may have had for her had obviously died the moment her father had forced this marriage on them. And could she blame him for that?

She had thought to explain to him, once the ceremony was over, that she was sorry for the part she had played in the outcome. Tell him that she had pleaded with her father, but that her da would not listen. And maybe then, maybe the two of them would be able to come to some kind of an accord.

But she had taken one look at the expression on Laird MacDonell's face when she had entered the kirk, and she knew that it mattered not what she had to say. He wanted naught to do with the marriage nor with her.

So she sat next to her new husband at the head table while their guests laughed and danced, and waved one of the serving maids over to refill her cup once more.

Her empty stomach rolled in protest, but she ignored the full plate of food that she had pushed away at the start of the night. The few small bites she had attempted to eat had tasted like ashes in her mouth.

Taking a long swallow of her wine, she closed her eyes as her head began to swim. With any luck she would be too drunk to remember her wedding night. Catriona shuddered at the thought. She did not think she could bear the man's touch. The thought of those hard eyes, so full of hatred, boring into her as she was forced to do her wifely duty in consummating the marriage made her want to run screaming from the hall.

She hastily took another sip of wine and set the cup down unsteadily on the table, causing some of the crimson liquid to spill out over her hand.

Next to her, Laird MacDonell stood up abruptly.

"I believe it is time we retired to bed, my lady," he snapped, extending her his hand.

Catriona's heart picked up its pace and the room spun. She was not ready! She reached again for her cup of wine, but her new husband took her by the arm and stopped her.

"I believe ye've had enough wine for the evening," he said as he pulled her out of the chair.

"I most certainly have not."

It was not until she glanced up and saw the dark look on his face that she knew she must have accidentally spoken out loud.

Her face burned, and she looked away from his disapproving gaze.

She squared her shoulders and allowed him to lead her from the wedding feast. When the guests noticed that they were leaving, a riotous cheer went up to send them on their way, and Catriona cringed at the sound.

As they crossed from the keep over to the mansion, Catriona felt as though she were being led to her own execution. Her feet felt weighted down with lead, and the air around her closed in on her, pressing against her so she felt as though she were forcing her way through a thick bog. When they reached the top of the stairs and were nearing the bedchamber in which The MacDonell was staying, Catriona's nerve failed, and her legs went weak, folding beneath her.

Suddenly she was dragged off her feet and gasped as Laird MacDonell hauled her up into his arms without saying a word.

When he turned right, away from his bedchamber door, Catriona looked up at him in confusion.

"Are we not…?" she trailed off, unsure of how to ask the question.

"Where is yer bedchamber?" he asked without looking down at her.

He carried her as though she weighed nothing. Her heart pounded as she wrapped her arms more securely around his neck. She was still afraid, but behind that fear, deep down, she felt an unbidden kernel of excitement.

Catriona felt strangely safe pressed up against the man's broad hard chest. The memory of it naked in the moonlight the night before rose in her mind, and her body flushed hot.

"'Tis another floor up still," she murmured. "Thank ye for helping me, but I can walk now."

Even as Catriona said the words, a part of her did not want him to set her back down.

He merely shook his head and continued on in silence.

She glanced up at him as subtly as she could, admiring the hard line of his jaw and wondered what he would look like if he ever smiled. She had been so afraid every time she was with him for one reason or the other, that she had never truly noticed how handsome a man he was.

His dark blonde hair curled lightly around his ears, and she suddenly found herself with the inexplicable urge to touch it. It was darker than her own pale locks, but had a hint of gold to it, almost like hay when the sun hits the fields just so. The wine coursing through her system had finally begun to make her feel at ease, and she allowed herself to relax into him.

Catriona tightened her arms around his neck and let out a wistful sigh. Maybe if they had met under different circum-stances, or had been allowed the time to get to know one another, he would not have hated her so much, and she would be headed to her marriage bed with her heart full of excitement and joy instead of fear. Not every woman was lucky enough to have a husband so handsome.

Unfortunately beauty did not make up for a lack of love or trust.

"It is this one here," she told him when they reached her chamber at last.

He opened the door and walked through it towards the bed, where he set her back down on her feet.

A large lump grew in Catriona's throat, making it hard for her to swallow. It was time.

"We leave in the morning," he said brusquely. "Good night, my lady."

Catriona watched open mouthed as Laird MacDonell turned his back on her and walked out of her bedchamber, closing the door behind him.

"But… what?" She sat down heavily on the edge of the bed and stared at the bedchamber door, unsure of what had just happened.

Liam's footsteps echoed down the empty hallway as he stormed away from Catriona's bedchamber. While in the great hall, surrounded by revelers, he had wished for nothing more than a single moment of peace and silence. But now that he had it, all he could think to wish for was a distraction. He needed something, anything, that would keep his mind from thinking about the way Catriona had just felt in his arms.

He did not want to think about the way her soft body had molded so perfectly against his, or the way it had made him feel when she had tightened her arms around his neck and rested her head again his chest. It had made him want to keep her close and protect her from harm, and aye, he had felt his lust stir as he gazed down on that sweet, heart-shaped face of hers. He wanted to know what it would feel like to gather that mass of silken pale blonde hair in his hands and let it slip through his fingertips, one smooth, shining lock at a time.

Liam scowled and shook his head in an attempt to clear the images from his mind.

No. It would take more than her sweet face and tempting curves to make him forget that the only reason he was carrying her in the first place was because of her clever deceit. No matter how tempting she was, he would not touch her until he knew for certain whether or not she had plotted with her father to trap him. Never again would he lay with a viper.

"Wandering the hallways on yer wedding night?"

His brother's voice snapped him to attention. Iain was leaning against the wall next to the door of Liam's chamber with a bottle of whiskey in one hand and two cups in the other.

"How did ye know I'd be here?"

"I know ye Liam, and I ken there was no way ye'd be bedding that lass tonight. I doubt ye'd want to give Laird Drummond the satisfaction. Or yourself." Iain winked and lifted the bottle in his hand. "As it turns out, Laird Drummond has quite the fine collection of spirits. I did not think he would mind if I helped myself to a bottle. It is a wedding, after all."

The keep was still full of wedding guests, and many of them had spilled out into the large courtyard, but Liam and Iain were able to slip past them unseen.

They walked past the stables and made their way around the manor house to the back. Behind the castle the land sloped downward in a green hill before ending in rough terrain.

"One of the serving maids said that Drummond plans to extend all of this into more elaborate gardens. What we see here is just the start. Everyone expects them to be the finest in all the highlands. She said he will be sparing no expense," Iain said.

"Is that supposed to impress me?" he asked. "That the man is willing to spend a fortune on a few posies?"

"No, but it's a nice thought. Of all the things the man could spend his money on, he chose to plant a garden."

"Ye have a poet's heart Iain. But I doubt very much that Laird Drummond wants to plant the most lavish garden in Scotland for any reason other than to be another display of his wealth and power."

"Must ye always be so cynical Liam?"

Liam looked back out over the vast expanse of green and gave a weary sigh.

"I dinna mean to be. Sometimes I wish that I was more like ye, do ye know that? But being Laird, it can weigh heavy on my heart whether I want it to or no'. And now with these new troubles…"

"Now that ye've wed his daughter, do ye think that ye can trust him to back ye with men if need be?"

"No matter what has happened here today, I have always heard that Drummond is a man of his word. I think that if the reaving is just the beginning and it turns out to be something more serious, we will be able to count on him to hold true."

"Well then at least this marriage will be of some use to ye."

"If it comes to war, her father's men are about the only use I have for her," Liam said bitterly, trying to erase the image of her that floated across his mind.

"She's quite bonny." Iain offered him the bottle of whiskey but Liam knew better than to drink any more that night. Riding with a splitting headache and a weak stomach after a night of too much spirits was something he wanted to avoid.

"Bonny or no, I've no use for a wife," Liam told him.

Iain chuckled and shook his head. "I'm sure I could think of a few uses for her."

"Ye're welcome to her then." Liam put his cup down on the low stone wall and turned to head back into the keep. "Be packed and ready to go by first light," he called over his shoulder. "Be sure the men know we will be leaving after breakfast. I am not going to spend another night under Laird Drummond's roof."

CHAPTER 6

THREE DAYS. Catriona shifted in the saddle, rocking gently from left to right and tried to release some of the tension in her lower back. Three days on horseback, but it was beginning to feel like three years.

Every muscle in her body ached. With each step her horse took, she was educated in new parts of her body of which she was previously unaware. Who knew those parts were even able to be sore? Spending the last two nights sleeping on the cold, hard ground had certainly not helped matters. And the tender bruise above her hip when she arose that morning was evidence that she must have rolled over and passed the better part of the night on top of a very hard rock.

Catriona scowled and bit the inside of her cheek to keep herself from screaming.

She and her sisters rarely traveled, but on the few occasions that they had, it had been much more comfortable, and had happened with considerably more planning. Never in her life would she have imagined herself sleeping out under the stars surrounded by the grunts and snores of men she hardly knew, with little more than her earsaid between her and the ground. The large woolen wrap, though favorable for warding off the cool night air, had done very little to soften the feel of the stony earth beneath her.

Laird MacDonell had not been exaggerating when he told her that they would be leaving on the morning after the wedding. She had only been allowed a few scant hours to pack her things, and had barely a moment to take in a few mouthfuls of breakfast before it had been time for her to say her tearful farewells.

The rest of her possessions were to be packed up and sent to her at the earliest opportunity, but for now she was expected to make do with little more than a few gowns and combs for dressing her hair. He had not even had the grace to allow her time to have a handmaid to accompany her. She prayed that there would be someone suitable for the position among his servants for her to choose from, otherwise she would have to beg her father to let her former maid make the journey to Invergarry Castle along with the rest of her possessions.

Catriona had hoped that once the two of them were away from her father, she and Laird MacDonell might get a chance to come to some type of peace, but she had obviously been a fool to hope for such a thing.

After spending this time with him on the road, it was clear to her now that her new husband was a man of ill humor, and his clansmen were no better. Laird MacDonell had spent the last three days barking orders at his men, and they in turn had leveled at her such looks of contempt that she had begun to both long for and dread the journey's end.

Never in her life had she felt more despised. The only one of The MacDonell clansmen to show her even a hint of kindness was, inexplicably, the Laird's own younger brother, Iain.

It was he, instead of her new husband, who brought her food, helped her with her bed roll, and assisted her with dismounting her horse. While the other men actively ignored her, Iain was quick with a smile and a joke to help lift her spirits. Catriona was certain that if it had not been for him, the journey to her new home would have been completely unbearable.

Catriona glanced over to where Iain rode next to her; a welcome buffer that stood between her and the unyielding man she had been forced to wed. The two brothers were similar in height, though Liam was more broad in stature. But where Liam's eyes were hard and cold when he looked at her, Iain's always seemed to sparkle with humor and mischief.

She couldn't help but wish that it had been Iain's bedchamber her father had caught her in. He seemed like the kind of man who would have allowed her to say her piece and would have forgiven her for her part in the unfortunate situation.

But Iain was not the man to which she had been wed, and no amount of wishing would make it so. She knew that dwelling on the impossible was not going to make her situation any easier.

Catriona watched as Laird MacDonell pulled ahead, and she scowled at his back. If the past three days had taught her anything, it was that the man was either determined to make her life miserable, or thought so little about her that she could ride her horse off the nearest cliff and he would never notice. Never before had she met a man so inconsiderate and unyielding.

"We are almost home, my lady," said Iain, pulling her from her thoughts. "See the castle, there?"

The thought of being able to climb down from her horse made the castle a welcome sight, and judging by the distance, it was only about an hour's ride away. But in no way did it feel like she was arriving home.

"Your home, perhaps," she told him, "but not mine."

"Aye, yours as well. It may not seem like it now, but ye'll come to love it in time."

"How can anyplace possibly feel like home when you are hated and shunned there?"

Iain followed her gaze to where Liam was riding ahead, and his smiled slipped a notch.

"Our people will not shun nor despise ye," he said gently.

"Why not, when it is so plain to see that their Laird does? Why should they respect me when he does not? None of the men riding with us do. Look around us, and ye'll see the truth of it."

"My brother can be difficult at times, I'll not be denying that. But I ask that ye be patient with him. He had never planned to wed again, so all of this comes as a shock to him. Give him time to come around to the idea of being married."

Catriona eyed her husband's back curiously. "He was wed before?"

Iain frowned and nodded, and Catriona noticed the usual openness and cheer had left his eyes. "Aye, he was."

When Iain did not say anymore, Catriona became even more curious.

"What was she like? Did he love her?" she asked. It was hard to picture Laird MacDonell as a loving husband, young and in love. What had happened to his first wife? Did he love her still? She stared at Liam, as countless questions tumbled through her mind. But one stood out among them all, what kind of woman must she have been to be able to capture his heart?

"If you want to know anything about my brother's first wife, ye're going to have to ask him. I'm sorry, lass, but that's for him alone to tell."

Catriona wanted to press him for more details but knew

that it would be of no use. Iain would not betray his brother's confidence simply to satisfy her curiosity.

"I dinna want him to hate me," she whispered.

Catriona could feel the tears beginning to well up in her eyes, and she quickly looked away from Iain so that he would not see. She did not want him to think her foolish or weak. And she did not trust that he would not tell his brother about it. She had her pride. She would not let her husband know just how deeply his ill treatment had affected her. If he would not even speak to her, and all he wanted was a cold and empty marriage, then that was exactly what he would get.

Invergarry Castle was smaller than her father's home, but still large and solidly built. A tight ball formed in Catriona's stomach as their party rode up to the keep and dismounted. The clansmen in the courtyard waved and cheered at their Laird's return, and Catriona suddenly felt as though she were surrounded. There was not a single familiar face in the crowd, and it struck her. She was alone.

Catriona watched the men dismount and waited patiently for Iain to come help her down, but when she looked around at the crowd, she could no longer see him.

"Give me yer hand, my lady."

Catriona turned, surprised to find Laird MacDonell standing next to her horse with his hand out waiting to assist her.

"I... Thank you, Laird MacDonell." She reached out hesitantly toward him, not entirely certain that he would not simply drop her on the ground when she least expected it. But he grasped her firmly by the waist and lifted her down off the horse in large, sure hands. He held her close, and her body slid along his until her feet were firmly on the ground. Every inch of her was going up in flames in the places where their bodies connected. They had not touched since their wedding night when he had carried her up to her bedchamber, and feeling the hard planes of his body brush against her now sent a bolt of excitement through her.

He did not release her immediately, and Catriona kept her hands pressed to his chest while she struggled to get her jagged breathing under control, without him noticing the effect that his touch had on her. But her mind struggled to comply, as focused as it was on the sensation of his strong hands gripping her waist.

She looked up into his face, and her heart sped up as he looked down at her. For the first time since the first night they had met, his eyes were not filled with anger at the sight of her, but instead, curiosity.

"Laird MacDonell," she said at last, her throat tight, "you may release me now."

She watched as his face clouded over, and he stepped back from her as if burned. Catriona wanted to kick herself. It was the first pleasant moment the two of them had shared, and she had somehow ruined it.

"Follow me, and I'll show ye to yer chamber," he said gruffly, and led her inside the keep.

Catriona tried to ignore the curious looks of the castle inhabitants as her husband led her through the hallways of the main keep and up to the bedchambers.

"Ye can have the chamber next to mine, for now. 'Tis the lady's chamber and has a connecting door to my own. Ye may keep it bolted or not, as ye like," he told her. He kept his voice light, and his face told her nothing of what he was feeling.

"Am I not to sleep in the same chamber as ye?" she asked, confused.

"Do ye really want to, lass?" he scoffed softly.

Catriona winced at the harshness in his voice, and admitted to herself that, no, she did not want to have to share a bed with this man. She cursed her earlier foolishness. How could her body react in such a way to someone she barely knew and who had nothing but contempt for her? Well, if he was not going to force himself on her, then she would gladly accept the blessing that she had been given.

"Thank ye, Laird MacDonell. This room will be fine."

She knew the moment the words were out of her mouth that she had somehow misspoken. His back straightened, and he was once again the cold indifferent man from before.

"I will send up what ye brought with ye today and make sure yer things are delivered to ye as soon as they arrive from yer father's home. No doubt yer tired from the long trip, so if ye'll excuse me, I have affairs to see to. Welcome to Invergarry Castle, *Lady* MacDonell."

He gave her a sharp bow and left her to fend for herself.

CHAPTER 7

LIAM LOOKED down at the pages of clan ledgers spread out before him and tried to focus on the thin columns. The numbers blurred on the page, and he sighed, slamming the ledger book shut and shoving the loose pages on his desk away from him in disgust. He could not focus with his mind constantly wandering to his new wife.

There was a sharp rapping on his study door and he looked up, but before Liam could answer, his youngest brother Alex stormed in, followed slowly by Iain.

"I doubt he is wanting to be disturbed," said Iain with a sigh.

"If what ye told me is true, then he is already disturbed," Alex snapped over his shoulder.

Liam sat back in his chair and crossed his arms over his chest. "So, Iain told ye, then."

"Aye, he told me. He told me that ye went and got yerself a wife that ye cannot even stand to look at, much less speak to."

Liam looked at Iain, surprised. "Ye told him that?"

Iain shrugged and dropped into one of the chairs across

from Liam and rested his boots up on the corner of the large desk with one ankle crossed over the other.

"He was bound to find out sooner or later. Ye dinna make much of an effort to hide yer dislike of the lass."

"Why would he like her? By the sounds of it she and her father tricked him into this. She sounds no better than Fiona."

"Alex…" Iain warned.

"Well is she?" Alex challenged him.

Iain nodded thoughtfully, "I think she is. And our brother would learn that for himself if he only gave the lass the chance to prove it."

"I gave her a chance, and she proved she wants naught to do with me," Liam said, flatly.

"Ye did?" said Iain, surprised. "When?"

"When I showed her to her chambers. I gave her a choice of sleeping in her own chamber or in mine and she chose to sleep in her own. The lass wants nothing to do with me."

Iain burst out laughing and shook his head.

"What?" Liam glared at him.

"Ye gave the lass a choice to be free from yer obvious dislike of her, and ye're surprised that she leapt at yer offer? Tell me, how quickly would *you* want to share a bed with someone that obviously hates ye? Yer distrust of the lass is making ye stupid Liam. The two of ye are in for a hard road if ye keep at it like this."

Iain stood and wiped the tears of laughter from his eyes.

"Yer a great leader and chief, brathaire, but ye've no idea how to romance a woman. The lass is all alone here. Unless ye really do want to spend the rest of your life suspicious of yer wife, I suggest ye at least try to get to know her. Who knows? Ye may actually find ye like her."

"This is madness," said Alex.

"Perhaps," said Iain, "but it is also too late to do anything about it."

Liam pinched the bridge of his nose, trying to suppresses the pain which was beginning to blossom in his forehead. "Do neither one of ye have anything better to do with yer time than harass me about the grim prospects of my marriage?"

"We do, in fact, have more pressing matters to discuss." Alex placed a pile of letters down in from of Liam and tapped the top page. "I received more reports of reaving along the border. They seem to me moving inward. Someone is attacking us, Liam, and something must be done."

Liam picked up the pile of reports and read through the top three before he sat back in his chair and threw the letters down in disgust. The thefts were happening more frequently. His brother was right, something was going to have to be done. If the farmers did not believe Liam could protect them, he would lose their respect and the respect of the rest of the clan.

"And still not a single witness," Liam growled in frustration.

Alex shook his head.

"All right. Alex I trust you to organize the patrols. I want these men caught and brought to me for questioning. I want to put a swift end to this. After three weeks it has gone on far too long. Ride out tomorrow. I am trusting ye to hunt these thieves down and bring them back to me so that they may meet justice."

"I will take care of it," said Alex. "Consider it done."

Liam stood and walked around the desk then placed a hand on Alex's shoulder and squeezed it tightly. I know ye will, *brathair beag*." At only twenty years, Liam's little brother was still filled with the exuberance of youth that Liam felt he himself had lost long ago. He knew that Alex wanted to prove himself a man in the eyes of his elder brothers and his chief. Sometimes it was hard for Liam to be one and the same. While Liam had responsibilities to The MacDonell clan, he also wanted to ensure that his brothers knew that he was always proud of them.

Their parents had died when Liam was only three and twenty. It was not long after his ill-fated marriage to Fiona. Some said that Liam had inherited the leadership of the clan too young, but for the past five years, The MacDonell's of Glengarry had prospered under his guidance. He was not about to let it all fall to ruin now.

"Come on. This will all be here waiting for us after supper." said Iain. "I'm hungry, and I look forward to sleeping in my own bed tonight." Iain eyed Liam slyly. "Now would be a fine time for ye to try to make peace with yer wife."

Liam scowled. "I highly doubt she wants much to do with me, Iain. I dinna doubt that if I were to invite her to dine with us this evening she would decline just to spite me. Perhaps ye could…"

Iain let out a weary sigh. "Christ almighty, Liam. Ye'd think ye were a green lad still in the schoolroom the way ye're carrying on. But aye, I'll go fetched yer wife for ye since ye've asked so nicely. Otherwise she's likely to starve."

"I have no plans to starve the lass," Liam grumbled.

"Maybe not, but it's plain to see that if it were left up to ye, the lass would probably still starve all the same."

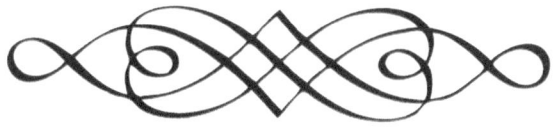

CHAPTER 8

LIAM SAT at the head table with the seat directly to the left of him conspicuously empty. Normally that was the seat Alex would occupy, but his youngest brother had vacated the position for Catriona. It may have been an empty gesture though, as Liam's new bride had still not arrived.

He glanced around the room and caught sight of Iain entering the great hall. His brother approached the head table slowly, the apprehension clear on his face.

"Where is she?" Liam asked him.

Iain hesitated for a moment before admitting, "She refuses to come down."

"What do you mean she refused to come down?" Liam's fingers tapped out an impatient tattoo on the tabletop next to his wine glass.

"She says that she is not hungry."

Liam could see the glint of amusement in his brother's eyes, but he did not find it the least bit funny. He was not about to have his new wife starve herself only to have the castles occupants gossip about his mistreatment of her.

Liam stood up from the table and began tossing roast

chicken and bread along with some vegetables carelessly onto one of the plates. Once the plate was filled to almost overflowing he marched silently out of the great hall and to Catriona's bedchamber.

"My lady?"

Liam knocked heavily on the door to Catriona's bedchamber and waited, but there was no answer.

"My lady?" he knocked again, louder this time.

"Catriona!" Liam started to get frustrated and considered letting himself into her chamber when the door opened at last.

"Laird MacDonell?" Catriona opened the door just wide enough to be able to look up at him. Liam's frustration was quickly replaced with concern. Her eyes were red and puffy, and her skin was chalky and pale. Had she been up here crying this whole time? Had Iain known?

"Ye did not come down for supper," he said awkwardly.

"I was not hungry," she whispered.

Liam lifted the plate of food for her to see. "I brought ye this in case ye change yer mind later."

Catriona eyed the over-filled plate for a moment before finally relenting, and opened the door wide enough to allow him entrance.

"Thank ye, Laird MacDonell," she whispered.

Liam set the plate down on the dressing table across from the bed and closed his eyes for a moment, taking a deep breath. He had done his duty, and she would not starve. There was really no reason for him to stay, but Iain's words continued to play over in his mind.

"I think that now we are married, ye should probably call me Liam."

"Thank ye for bringing me my supper... Liam."

He turned around to look at her, properly look her for the first time since the night they had met. Catriona stood in the middle of the room with her eyes downcast focused on the floor. There was no air of triumph about her, no victory. The dark circles under her eyes betrayed her exhaustion, but was that her fatigue from the journey to Invergarry, or the crying she had so obviously been doing before he had arrived?

Maybe Iain had the right of it after all. Catriona was well and truly alone here. And if she had, in fact, not schemed with her father to force him to wed her, then he was forcing the lass to suffer for no reason other than his own stubborn pride. He had not even given her a chance to tell her own side of it.

"I'm sorry if I've been cruel to ye, lass," he said, softly. "I did not mean to upset ye."

Catriona instantly squared her shoulders and lifted her chin. Liam watched as her eyes narrowed in suspicion, and he felt like a great hulking beast. Had he really treated her so poorly over the past few days that she now could not trust a few simple words of kindness from him?

"I understand if ye do not wish to hear my apology…" He trailed off, at a loss for words. Iain was the one that always ken what to say. Liam was used to speaking plainly and to other men. He did not know how to soothe an irate wife.

"I accept yer apology, Laird MacDonell… Liam. If that is all, ye may go now."

Frustrated, Liam took two steps toward the door, and then stopped.

"I want to trust ye lass, I do. But I dinna like being tricked into marriage. I never wanted this."

The color raised in Catriona's cheeks, and her eyes were like sharp daggers cutting through him.

"And ye think I wanted this, is that it?" she asked. Her voice was devoid of all emotion as she stepped toward him.

Catriona tilted her head back so that she could look Liam

in the eye. She may have been a good head and shoulders shorter than him, but her glare suddenly made him feel as though he were a man of half his stature.

"I'll have ye know, Liam MacDonell, that I did not want to marry ye either. I begged my father, pleaded with him to release ye. I tried to convince him that ye were not the one who attacked me, but he would not listen. There was nothing I could do. Do ye really think that given a choice, I would choose to be here with ye? To be brought to a place without friends or family, and wed to a man that pays me so little regard that he has only spoken a handful of words to me the entire time we have been wed? A man so devoid of humor that I have yet to see him smile? A man who, every time he looks at me, has eyes so filled with suspicion and derision that it is all I can do to stand my ground and not look away? Tell me, *Laird MacDonell*, why would I ever scheme to trick a man like that into marrying me? What woman with even the smallest amount of wits would choose to wed herself to someone so cold and unfeeling?"

Her words cut to the very heart of him. His emotions warred between the great feelings of relief that washed over him, because he could hear the truth in her words that she had not wanted to marry him, and the frustration that now he knew he could trust her, she wanted absolutely nothing to do with him. He wanted to apologize to her once again, but she continued on before he had a moment to recover.

"I do not know why ye were so quick to judge me guilty of some imagined crime. Perhaps it had something to do with yer previous wife. But I have taken more than I can stomach of yer suspicion and insults."

Liam reached out and grabbed Catriona by the upper arms and pulled her closer. All thought of apologizing fled his mind at the mention of his first wife.

"Where did ye hear about my first marriage? Who told ye about Fiona?" He demanded.

Catriona's eyes widened in fear, and she struggled against him.

"It was Iain," she snapped. "Who else could it have been? Yer brother is the only one of ye to have shown me even the least bit of kindness. Now unhand me!" She tore herself out of his grasp and took a hasty step back.

"Husband or no, I will not be manhandled by the likes of ye, Liam MacDonell! Ye are a terror and a brute, and I wish I had been married to yer brother instead!" she shouted.

A hard knot formed in Liam's stomach, and he snorted in derision. It was not the first time a woman would prefer to be with his brother instead of him. Liam thought that the sting of it had lessened over time, but for some reason, knowing that his new wife would have preferred to be married to his brother stung more than he wanted to admit.

"Oh, aye, well, all the lasses prefer Iain, and Iain has had affections for many a pretty lass. I would suggest ye spend some time getting to know my brother before ye start dreaming him up to be some gallant prince, lass. Especially if ye have hopes for a husband that will not stray far from yer marriage bed," he added, cruelly.

Catriona blushed furiously but held her ground. "That may be so, but at least he has shown some concern for me. Whereas all ye've shown is how little ye want to do with me. Ye dinna even want me to share yer bedchamber!"

Catriona froze the moment the words were out of her mouth and she whirled around, turning her back on him.

Liam's heart pounded as he tried to decider Catriona's meaning.

"Are ye saying that ye want to share a bedchamber with me then?" he asked.

"No, of course not!"

"Of course not," he mimicked harshly. "Why would ye want to share a bedchamber with me when ye've been dreaming of yer shining knight Iain MacDonell?"

Catriona's fists clenched at her sides, and she turned back around to face him.

"I have *not* been dreaming of Iain. Why must ye twist my words?"

"Ye've already admitted that he would rather be married to him than me—"

"But that does not mean…! Oh! Why must ye be so infuriating!" Catriona shouted.

"Well if I'm infuriating, at least I'm in good company, lass!" Liam crossed his arms over his chest and stared at her pointedly.

"Oh!" Catriona stormed over to the door and held it open. "Thank ye very much for bringing me supper, Laird MacDonell, but I have grown overtired. I think it is past time for ye to leave."

Liam raised his eyebrows at her but didn't budge.

"Are ye trying to force me out of a chamber in my own keep?"

"Of course not," she said with all the dignity she could manage, but her eyes betrayed that she recognized the absurdity of the situation. "But I'm sure that as a gentleman ye'll respect my wishes and go."

"Oh I'm a gentleman now then, am I?" The corner of Liam's mouth twitched as he fought to control a smile. "I thought ye were just telling me what a great unfeeling brute I am?"

Liam did not know why he continued to bait her, but seeing Catriona standing there with her back straight and the color high in her cheeks as she fought to keep her temper under control suddenly made him want to laugh.

"Are ye mocking me?" she snapped at him.

"Of course not." Liam shook his head but could not keep his shoulders from trembling.

"Ye are so! Ye're laughing at me!" she said, obviously outraged.

"I am not, Catriona, I swear it." Unfortunately his body betrayed him as a liar, and unable to control himself any longer, Liam threw his head back and roared with laughter.

"It's not funny!" Catriona shouted as she stared at him. "Have ye completely lost yer wits?"

Liam leaned against the table and let the laughter consume him. It was all he could do with the absurdity of the situation. With every passing day it felt as though more and more was slipping out of his control, and now… this.

As Catriona stood there watching him her shoulders too began to shake, and soon she was laughing so hard that tears were streaming down her face.

"This is absolutely… absurd!" she gasped, stumbling forward to collapse on the bed.

"I ken, lass," Liam agreed.

He sat down beside her as he tried to get his breath, then very slowly, took one of her hands in his own. "I ken ye dinna like me very much," he said gently. "And I ken I have not given ye much of a reason to. But, I think we can agree that what is done is done, aye? And maybe, in time, the two of us can come to a peace?"

Catriona looked down at their joined hands and then up into his eyes.

"I think that I would like that," she told him. "In truth, I was not sure how much longer I would have been able to stand it if ye went on hating me. While I knew it was unlikely I would ever get to marry for love, I had hoped that my future husband and I would at least share some affection, and friendship."

Liam squeezed her hand gently and she smiled at him. It

was the same open smile that he had seen her give his brother on the journey to Invergarry Castle. He tried to suppress the swift wave of jealousy that rose in him at the thought of his brother and tried to focus on the fact that now, he and Catriona might have a chance at an amicable marriage after all.

"I should leave ye to yer supper and get some rest," he said, releasing her hand and getting to his feet.

He noticed Catriona's smile slip a notch and a spike of pleasure went through him. She wanted him to stay.

"Tomorrow I can take some time and show ye around the keep... If ye like."

"I dinna suppose..." she trailed off and bit her bottom lip.

Watching her, Liam was suddenly struck with the desire to do that very same thing. And in that moment he wanted nothing more than to bend down and nibble on Catriona's bottom lip.

"Aye?" he asked, his voice gruff and his eyes not leaving her mouth.

"I dinna suppose there are any paints in the keep? I dropped mine the night of... the night we met, so have not brought any with me. I like to paint, and it will help me to pass the time."

Liam could not think of a single person that might have paints in the keep, but he wanted nothing more than to see her smile again.

"Dinna worry, I can find ye paints."

CHAPTER 9

CATRIONA RAN her hands over her sides and tried to smooth out the non-existent wrinkles in her lavender gown. It was plain vanity, she admitted to herself, which made her choose that specific gown over the others. The color brought out the blue in her eyes, making them appear both larger and more intense in color. She had carefully dressed her hair in a single plait swept to one side and brought down over the front of her shoulder which she had fastened with a lavender ribbon that matched her gown. She turned to the left and right, trying to assess herself in the mirror. Though her hands were steady, she could not deny the slight fluttering sensation deep in the pit of her stomach. She wanted the day to go well. It was a chance for her and Liam to make a fresh start. Was it possible that there was a flicker of hope for their marriage after all?

Catriona took a deep breath, followed by another, and tried to calm the fluttering in her stomach. It was ridiculous for her to feel so ill at ease. She had not gone down to the great hall for breakfast, feeling too unwell to eat, and she hoped that Laird MacDonell... nay, that *Liam*, did not misinterpret that as a sign she had changed her mind. She was looking forward to him showing her around the keep and introducing her to her new home.

Catriona smiled and tucked a loose strand of hair behind her ear. For the first time since she found out she was coming to Invergarry Castle, she finally felt as though it could be a home to her one day. She and Liam had taken the first steps towards an accord between the two of them, and she wanted to make sure she did all that she could for them to continue on in the right direction.

She wiped her damp palms against the soft woven fabric of her gown and paced the length of the chamber while she waited. *I wonder what he would do if I simply left to go find him?*

It was not as if she had been confined to the space. There was nothing stopping her from leaving and venturing out to hunt down her new husband on her own. The more she thought about it, the more annoyed she became. It was unfair of him to keep her waiting like this.

There was a quick rap on the door, and all feelings of annoyance were quickly replaced by those of anticipation. She couldn't help but wonder if he would take her hand again, the way he had the night before. She never would have guessed that he would be so gentle with her. His carrying of her up the stairs on their wedding night most certainly did not count. Though she still warmed at the memory of what it felt like to have his strong arms wrapped around her and the hard lines of his broad chest against her cheek.

"Good morning," Catriona said as she hurried to open the door. "I have spent all morning looking forward to ye showing me around the—Iain!" she finished, surprised to be looking up into his devilish face.

"Ye flatter me, my lady," he said to her with an easy smile and a wink.

Catriona blushed furiously, not only for his comment, but

for the things she had said to Liam the night before. She couldn't believe she had said such things to her husband about his own brother. She eyed him as he stood outside her door, and wondered if Liam had told his younger brother what she had said about him.

"That is not what I meant," she hurried to explain. "I was just surprised to see ye. I have been expecting—"

"Liam, aye, I know. My brother has sent me to ye with his apologies. He has been called away from the keep for the day by his duties as Chief. I am to pass on his message to ye that he is sorry he did not have time to bid ye a proper farewell. But as he had to leave before breakfast he also did not want to wake ye." Iain leaned against the doorframe and smiled at her. "He said that he had promised to show ye around the castle today and asked me to take ye in his stead. I know that I'm a poor substitute, but I hope ye have no objections?"

Catriona could not help but laugh at Iain's false modesty. She could not think of a single man, woman or child that would object to spending time with Iain MacDonell. But she could not quell the flicker of disappointment she felt at his arrival. Of course she understood the pressures Liam was under as chief of his clan. She had grown up seeing just how many responsibilities her father shouldered. But even though she knew Liam hadn't a choice in being called away, Catriona found herself disappointed all the same.

"I would love for ye to be my guide and escort today, Iain, thank ye." Catriona tried to not let her disappointment show. "But are ye sure I would not be taking ye away from something more important?"

"Spend my morning locked up in my brother's moldy study, or strolling the grounds accompanied by his lovely new wife? Nay, I know when to take advantage of a fine opportunity."

He extended her his elbow, and Catriona linked her arm

through his. Liam or no, it was time for her to step out of the shadows and acquaint herself with her new home.

"I dinna suppose there is a pond or anything of the like nearby is there?" She asked him as they headed towards the staircase.

"Aye, we've a loch not far from here. Why do ye ask?"

"I think that once I am more settled, I would like to paint the water."

"Ye're an artist?"

"I dinna think I would go so far as to say that, but I do love to paint and draw, aye."

"Liam used to sketch when he was younger."

Catriona was so stunned by that news, she missed a step, and Iain had to hold tight to her so that she did not fall.

"Really?" she asked as she clung to his arm. She would never have imagined that they would have such a thing in common. Why had he not mentioned it the night before, when she had asked him about the paints?

"I dinna think he has drawn anything in years, but when he was younger he had quite the fair hand. Maybe he will draw ye something if ye ask him."

"Thank ye, Iain. I think I will."

Iain and Catriona sat on a blanket on the grassy edge of Loch Oich, gazing out across the water as it sparkled in the afternoon sun. The water rippled gently from the cool spring breeze, and Catriona wrapped her earasaid more tightly around her shoulders to ward off the chill.

"Would ye like to go back?" Iain asked, noticing her shiver.

"No, thank ye. The loch is so beautiful, thank ye for bringing me here. I canna wait to paint it."

"Did ye bring yer paints with ye to the keep?"

Catriona shook her head sadly. "No. I lost them the night I… the night I met yer brother. Liam promised that he would try to find some for me." Catriona smiled softly and looked away.

"It is nice to see the two of ye speaking at last."

"I must admit that I was not so sure that the day would come. But it is nice to know that he does not hate me, at the very least," she said softly.

"I'm sure there have been many a fine marriage built on less than that."

Catriona was saved the need to come up with an answer by the sound of hoofbeats behind them. She turned to see a large brown horse bearing down on them from across the glen. As the horse grew nearer she could clearly make out the large form of Liam atop the stallion.

Her head cocked to the side as she watched him draw nearer. He was an impressive sight. His large stature made him an imposing figure as he easily commanded the large beast beneath him to draw to a halt a few feet from where she and Iain sat.

Liam swung down off of his horse and strode toward them carrying a large wooden box under his arm.

"Good day to ye, Catriona," Liam said, inclining his head to her.

"Liam." Catriona could feel her face growing warm and tucked a loose strand of hair behind her ear.

"I'm sorry that I could not escort ye around the keep today. I hope the two of ye have had a pleasant time."

Catriona smiled brightly. "Yes, yer brother was an excellent guide. I hope yer day was as pleasant as ours?"

"I doubt it was as pleasant as yours, but I'm glad to see that my brother kept ye good company."

She shifted uncomfortably, remembering her words from

the previous night. She could not deny that Iain made for pleasant company, but she wanted to get to know her new husband. She was happy that Liam was trying to make her feel more comfortable in her new home, but the thought of ever feeling as at ease with him as she did with Iain felt like an impossible dream.

Liam sat down beside her on the wool blanket with his legs crossed and his knee brushed against her thigh. The contact made her skin flush, and she looked away from him, out across the deep water of the loch.

"Well," said Iain, getting to his feet, "I have some business of my own that I should be seeing to. I'll leave ye now, Lady Catriona, in yer husband's care."

"Thank ye for taking the time to show me around the grounds today, Iain." She smiled warmly at him.

Iain bowed deeply and winked. "It was my pleasure. I look forward to seeing the both of ye at supper tonight."

"Aye, Iain, we will be seeing ye there," Liam said.

Catriona couldn't help but notice a hint of impatience in his voice, and smiled inwardly. Could it be that he had been looking forward to spending some time together just as much as she had been?

"What is that?" she asked Liam, eyeing the box he had set down on the other side of him.

He smiled at her and handed her the box he had brought with him.

"Why don't ye open it and see for yourself?"

Catriona took the box from him and placed it gently on her lap. Her hands trembled slightly as she lifted the lid to reveal a beautiful paint set. Inside were charcoal sticks for sketching and small pots of paints filled with different colors along with a large stack of drawing paper that was tied with a white ribbon.

"Oh Liam, it's absolutely beautiful," she gasped, trailing

her fingers gently over each item in the box. "Wherever did you find it? When did you have the time?"

Liam, gave a light shrug and cleared his throat. "I promised ye that I would look for paints…" he trailed off for a moment before finally asking hesitantly, "Do ye like them, then?"

With a laugh Catriona threw her arms around his neck and hugged him close. "I absolutely love them! Oh Liam, it is such a thoughtful gift. Thank you, they're perfect."

Liam shifted awkwardly, caught off guard by Catriona's unexpected show of affection. Slowly, he raised his arms and wrapped them lightly around Catriona's waist.

At the touch of his hands upon her, Catriona froze, suddenly aware of the intimacy of their embrace. Embarrassed by her sudden outburst, she began to pull away from him, but Liam's grip on her prevented her from making much space between them.

Halted by his grip, she stopped her retreat, her face now mere inches from his. She found herself staring at the fullness of his lips. She had never before noticed how inviting they looked. Most likely because they had always been curled into some form of frown or scowl whenever he was looking at her.

Catriona glanced upwards and was caught in the gaze of Liam's stormy grey eyes. Suddenly, one of Liam's hands was in her hair, and he pulled her closer to him. His mouth met hers, and she inhaled deeply, shocked by the unexpected kiss.

The movement of his lips were tentative at first, as though he were asking a question, and Catriona yearned for more. More of what, she didn't quite understand, but she knew that she did not want to dampen the smoldering need that was growing inside from the kiss he pressed upon her.

She whimpered lightly, hungry for something that she couldn't quite identify, but the sound must have spurred

Liam on, because his lips instantly became more insistent. He kissed her harder, and his tongue flicked over her lips, teasing its way into her mouth.

Catriona clung to him, reveling in the new sensations flooding her body. And then just like that, Liam pulled back, and the kiss was over just as quickly as it had started.

"We should be getting back to the keep," Liam said. His voice was gruff, but his hand was gentle as he pushed the hair back from her face.

Catriona blushed, but nodded silently, allowing Liam to help her to her feet. Her lips still tingled from his kiss, and as he lifted her onto her horse, she hoped that it would not be long before he kissed her again.

CHAPTER 10

SHE WAS GOING to be late. Catriona rushed down the hallway towards the great hall where most of the castle inhabitants had already begun to gather for supper. She had taken extra time redressing her hair for the evening meal. She had to admit that she wanted to look beautiful for Liam. It seemed a bit silly, worrying so much that the sight of her would be pleasing to him. But every time she thought about the kiss they had shared earlier on the banks of Loch Oich, her face warmed, and she ached for him to take her into his arms and kiss her again. It was no secret that men wanted to kiss beautiful women. Growing up, she had often overheard the maids giggling about the young men and so...

She shook her head. It was silly to even think about. But she wanted to be beautiful tonight in hopes that it would make him want to kiss her again.

But more importantly, tonight she would be introduced to the gathered clansmen as Liam's new wife, Lady MacDonell, and she wanted to make a good impression on her new clansmen as well.

As she rushed around a corner, she slammed into someone coming the other way.

"Oh!" she exclaimed, "My apologies, I was not paying close enough attention to where I was going."

"It is I who should be apologizing," he said. "In my rush, I could have knocked ye down."

Catriona looked up at the man who had a firm grip on her arm. He was tall, almost as tall as Liam, but narrower through the shoulders and had wavy light brown hair. As Catriona gazed at him, she saw his deep brown eyes focusing on her and narrow slowly as he examined her face.

"I do not believe we have met before," he said, his voice suddenly more cool and suspicion.

"No, I have not been at Invergarry Castle for long." Her heart beat rapidly. Why was he so suspicious of her?

"And what might your name be, lass?"

"Lady Catriona MacDonell. Now I'll ask ye to unhand me."

The hand on her upper arm tightened, and she flinched from the pressure. She tried to pull herself from his grasp, but he did not release her.

"So, you are the one who married my brother," he said coolly.

"You are Liam's brother?" Catriona should have felt comforted by that fact, but she was not. The undisguised expression of dislike on his face made it clear that she was not welcome.

"Ye have some nerve, showing yer face here after what ye have done."

"I did not do anything. Now, let me go. Yer brother is expecting me."

"Did not do anything? Ye tricked my brother into marrying ye, and ye consider that no little thing?"

"I do not know what you think happened between yer

brother and me, but I did not trick him into marriage. I think it would be best for you to speak to your brother. Now please, I am late."

"Let me tell you what I know. I know that I am not going to let you ruin my brother's life."

Catriona was rapidly growing irritated with Liam's brother's accusations.

"I have no intention of doing any such thing. And I have no interest in discussing this with you further. Now please let me pass."

Alex leaned in, crowding Catriona and lowered his voice. "Ye do not belong here," he said menacingly.

"What is going on here?"

Alex took a step back at the sound of Iain's voice. "Nothing," he said. "I am simply getting acquainted with our brother's new bride."

Iain eyed his younger brother suspiciously, unconvinced by his claim.

"Catriona, do you mind if I speak to Alex for a moment?"

"Of course not." Catriona sighed with relief, grateful of the escape she had been offered.

She slipped away from Alex and flashed Iain a small smile as she passed him. She had not gone far when she heard Iain addressing his brother behind her back.

"What do ye think ye are doing?"

"I've no idea what ye mean," Alex said casually.

Catriona glanced back to see him lean against the wall and cross his arms over his chest, a bored expression on his face. She started down the stairs but paused once she was out of sight.

"Ye know exactly what I mean. Not even a blind man would have mistaken that look in your face as one of welcome."

"It wasn't, because she's not. She doesn't belong here Iain, ye know it as well as I do."

"She's Liam's wife, this is her home now. The faster ye come to terms with that, the easier it will be on everyone."

"Why are ye defending her?"

"Because I've actually taken the time to speak to her. She's a sweet lass."

"Ye've always had a soft spot when it comes to the ladies. She's blinded ye with her charms."

"No, yer suspicion of her has blinded ye to seeing what's right in front of yer face. That this could be our brother's chance at happiness. Don't come between them by making her feel uncomfortable."

"Ye cannot ask me to trust her."

"All I'm asking is that ye keep a civil tongue in your mouth when ye speak to her. What's done is done. She and Liam are wed. So just keep your opinions on the matter to yourself and let the two of them make a go of it."

Alex snorted. "Have ye always been this much of a bleeding heart, or are ye just getting soft in your old age."

"I simply know that no good will come of ye sticking yer nose where it doesn't belong."

"So says you."

"Aye, I do. So do ye promise to not go stirring up trouble?"

"No. But I promise to hold my tongue at least until after supper. Come on, before Liam starts to wonder where we are."

Hearing their footsteps approach her, she rushed down the staircase before they could discover her and realize that she had been eavesdropping. She was grateful to Iain for defending her, but she had also learned something important. That she needed to keep out of Alex's way the best she could if she wanted to avoid more unpleasant confrontations with him in the future.

Catriona could feel every eye in the great hall on her. She sat silently next to Liam, trying to ignore, not only the weight of the stares that she felt from everyone in the room, but also the not-so-subtle glares from Alex, who was seated next to her on her right.

Liam pushed back his seat and stood up from the table, his glass raised as he introduced Catriona to his clansmen as his new wife, but she did not hear a word of it. She was trying as hard as she could to block out the cruel words Alex was whispering to her under his breath.

"Ye may have my brothers fooled, but I know ye for the deceitful wee bitch ye truly are, and I dinna care what it takes, I'll find the proof of it and expose ye to my brothers."

Catriona squeezed her hands together beneath the table and fought the urge to slap Liam's brother. She could not take much more of the poison he was spewing into her ear.

"Ye may sit there, looking all innocent, but I see right through ye. And my fellow clansmen will see through ye as well. I dinna ken why ye did it, and I dinna care, but ye'll not get away with this."

"Please," she whispered, unable to hear any more, "just stop."

"I'll not stop until ye're out from under this roof. I'll have ye gone, even if I have to drag ye out of here by yer hair myself."

The room broke into thunderous applause, pulling Catriona's attention back to Liam. He had finished his speech and was looking down at her expectantly. A moment passed before she realized that he was expecting her to say something.

Hurriedly, she stood up from her chair and forced a smile to her lips, as she looked around the room. She did not want to focus on any of the faces, afraid of the expressions she would see cast back at her. Terrified that they, like Alex, would be filled with suspicion and hostility. But as she stood there looking down at them, though some people were eyeing her with open curiosity, the residents of Invergarry Castle looked genuinely happy to see their Laird wed. Bolstered by this, she pushed aside the thoughts of Alex's threats and found the courage to speak.

"Thank ye, husband. I am so happy to be here. And thank ye all for welcoming me so warmly to Invergarry Castle. It is already starting to feel like home."

She took her seat quickly as the inhabitants applauded once more, and Liam caught her eye, raising a questioning eyebrow at her.

She blushed and shrugged her shoulder slightly. It was a pretty lie, and each one of them at the head table knew it, but what else was she to say? That she would give anything to be back at her father's house, laughing with her sisters? No. She and Liam had agreed to move forward in harmony, and she would honor her word. This was her life and her home now.

"Look how easily ye lie. Ye give yourself away," said Alex as he reached for his whiskey.

Catriona could take no more. She pushed back her seat and rose abruptly from the table.

"Catriona?" Liam asked.

"I'm sorry, Liam. If ye'll excuse me."

Alex relaxed casually in his chair, a satisfied smirk on his lips as he sipped his drink. She shook with anger, wanting nothing more than to strike him as she fought back the tears that burned at her eyes.

Iain leaned over and whispered something in Liam's ear as Catriona turned and left the head table, hurrying towards the doors of the great hall. All she wanted was to get as far away from Alex as possible.

As soon as she was out of the great hall, she collapsed against the nearest wall and started to cry, unable to hold back the tears any longer.

"Catriona?" Liam said.

She jumped in surprise. She had been crying so hard that she had not even heard him approach her.

"Oh!" Hastily, she rubbed the back of her hands across her eyes, trying to wipe away the tears, but it was of no use. For every tear she brushed away, more fell, until she simply gave up trying to hide it completely. She buried her face in her hands and sobbed. Now that she had started, she was simply unable to stop.

"Catriona, what is it?"

Liam rested a tentative hand on her shoulder, and squeezed it gently. "I know that ye're not happy here. But I thought... Is there something that I can do for ye?"

Catriona shook her head.

"Is it really so horrible here as all that?" His voice was soft and filled with concern.

She looked up at him and saw the worry and guilt in his eyes. She was torn. She did not want to come between Liam and his brothers. Would he even believe her if she told him the cruel things that Alex had said?

"I dinna know how to explain."

Liam took her by the shoulders and turned her towards him. "Take yer time lass, and tell me what's troubling ye. Is it me? Have I done something to upset ye?"

"It's not you."

"Then what is it lass?"

"It's Alex," she whispered.

He frowned at her, and she wished she could take it back. "Has he said something to upset ye?"

She nodded, but said nothing. Liam stared down at her, waiting silently for her to continue.

"He does not trust me. And I suppose that I cannot blame him for that. But he keeps saying such horrible things. I tried to tell him that you and I had made peace with our situation, but he said that he would see me gone from the castle if he had to drag me out of here himself. He hates me, and I dinna think he is going to stop."

Liam's face was expressionless as he released Catriona and walked back into the great hall without a word. She stood alone, her stomach tied in anxious knots, cursing herself for telling him what Alex had done. He obviously didn't believe her, or didn't care, otherwise why would he have simply walked away from her like that? Did he think that she was trying to turn him against his brother?

A few minutes later Alex stormed out of the great hall with Liam close behind him. Catriona froze when Alex caught sight of her and headed in her direction, his face red with anger.

"Ye may have him fooled," he said, jabbing his finger toward her face, "but it will not last." He looked over his shoulder with a sneer and shook his head. "Ye're an idiot brathair. I just hope I can convince ye of that before it's too late."

Catriona wrapped her arms around herself and watched Alex storm off.

"Whatever did ye say to him?" she asked Liam.

"I told him that I would not have him speaking to my wife with disrespect, and that if he could not keep a civil tongue in his head around ye, then I would not have him around ye. We've been having some troubles with reaving on our lands the past few months and it's been getting worse. That's why I was visiting with yer father in the first place, ye ken. I've sent Alex off to join the search to find the thieves. He was meant to be leaving soon at any rate. I've simply hurried him on his way."

Catriona was stunned. Had Liam actually sent his brother away for her? She could hardly believe what she was hearing.

"Ye sent him away... for me?"

Liam glanced at her and then looked away, clearing his throat. "Aye, well. I am yer husband, no?"

She nodded, staring at him silently, still not sure she fully believed what had just happened.

"Thank you," she said at last.

Liam took her hand in his and, without another word, led her back into the great hall.

CHAPTER 11

EARLY MORNING LIGHT spilled across the small sitting room. The soft beams struck Catriona, played with the colors of her hair, and illuminated her in a gentle halo. Liam marveled at the way the pale strands glowed in the sunlight as they tumbled carelessly down her back in a riotous waterfall of waves.

Her hand moved swiftly across the large page in sweeping arcs, her attention focused solely on the image unfolding before her. She had yet to notice his presence, and Liam held himself as still as possible, watching her from the doorway, not wanting to break her concentration.

He had not shown her this room, but he was not surprised to find that she had been drawn to it once she found it. On the fifth floor of the keep, the windows in this sitting room were overlarge and granted a sweeping view of the loch below. It had been his mother's favorite place in the entire keep. Two chairs flanked the hearth, which was now cold, but in winter would warm the entire room, and in his mother's time would fill it with a delicious scent, as she would set a pot filled with her secret blend of spices over the flame. Even now, he could still see his mother stirring the pot to fragrance the air while he watched her, munching on sweet bread.

Shifting his weight, he accidentally bumped into the door frame, shattering the peaceful tableau. Catriona's hand froze, her head snapping in his direction.

"Liam!"

"I'm sorry, I did not mean to disturb ye." The relaxed air that she had about her was gone. No longer filled with sharp concentration, her eyes were guarded and unsure as she looked at him, filling him with regret for intruding upon what small sanctuary she had created for herself.

"Did ye have need of me?"

He shook his head and took a tentative step into the room. He had lived in the keep his entire life and knew every last stone and beam, but stepping into that room, he could not help but feel as though he were stepping out of his home and into her domain. A sacred space in which he had no right to be.

"Nay, I was merely passing when I saw ye, and I..." What? How could he possibly explain to her that he was so capti-vated by the sight of her that he could merely stop and stare. He felt foolish just thinking about it.

"What are ye drawing?" he asked, hoping to change the direction of the conversation.

Catriona tilted the page away from him so that he was unable to make out the image she was creating there.

"It is nothing, really."

A sharp bolt of rejection ran through him. She obviously did not want to share her art with him. It felt as though she was locking him out of her world.

"I want to apologize for not spending much time with you over the past few days. I have not meant to ignore ye.

There have just been so many things that have been needing my attention."

Her eyes shifted away from him to gaze out the window, but he could still see the disappointment in her eyes.

"I understand, Liam. I am sure that as Laird, there is much that needs yer constant attention. Ye need not worry about me. I am more than capable of finding ways to pass the time on my own."

How many hours had she sat alone in this room over the past week? He mentally kicked himself. The lass must have been going out of her mind with boredom and loneliness.

"Catriona...." He knelt next to her and tried to take her hand, but she grasped her papers more tightly. He grasped her wrist awkwardly, unsteadily. "I'm so sorry, lass. I constantly seem to be failing ye."

She looked at him then, but far from the anger he expected, her eyes were filled with kindness and warmth.

"Yer not failing me, Liam. I just thought..." She blushed, her gaze flickering down to his lips for a moment before they met his gaze once more. "I just thought that we would be spending more time together."

Her blush deepened and Liam stared into her eyes, conjuring a memory of the way her soft body felt when he held her on the banks of the loch.

"Aye." His throat was tight as he admired the soft plump bow of her lip. "We should be spending more time together." Unbidden, his hand floated up to her face, and his thumb brushed across her bottom lip as if of its own accord. Her eyes fluttered closed at his touch, and she leaned forward into his caress.

It amazed him that he ever thought her to be the same as his first wife. The difference between them was clear to anyone with eyes. No wonder Iain thought him so foolish.

Catriona was warm and understanding, and welcomed his touch.

He caressed her cheek and she tilted her head slightly, pressing it into his cupped palm. His heart pounded as he leaned forward and closed the distance between them. He kissed her roughly, forcing her mouth open and plumbing the sweet depths of it with his tongue. Through the haze of his lust, he heard her gasp, caught off guard by his assault, but he did not stop. He could not. He ached to lose himself in the sweet innocence of her touch. To cast aside the doubt and guilt that he felt whenever he looked at her. Because kissing her now, he could finally admit, that it was not duty alone that had kept him from her side. It was this. It was the spark of hope he felt when she was near. A hope that he was not yet ready to embrace, for fear that she could still turn on him.

He gathered her hair in his hands and continued his assault on her mouth, urged on by her soft moans. He ached to lose himself in her. To drown in the scent of her and be freed from the weight and pain of his past that he carried on his back like scars.

With his free hand, he reached up under her skirts and caressed her calf and stroked up the outer side of her thigh. He grasped it tightly, his fingers digging into her creamy flesh, and he felt a shudder go through her. His fingers slid towards her inner thigh, when suddenly, he felt her entire body go rigid. Her lips stopped moving, and it pulled him from his need-driven haze.

Panting heavily, he rested his head against her shoulder and squeezed his eyes shut, struggling to regain control of himself. Slowly, he released Catriona's thigh and slid his hand from beneath her gown.

"Liam?" Her voice was tentative, unsure, and Liam winced at the slight quiver he heard there.

He slowly raised his head, and braced himself for her fear and disgust. What had he been thinking, assaulting his wife in broad daylight, with the door wide open where anyone could have passed and seen them?

Catriona's face was flushed, and her chest rose and fell in quick succession. Her soft, smooth hair was a tangled mess where his hand was in it moments ago, and her swollen red lips looked tender and sore.

"I'm sorry," she said. "I just…"

Liam wrapped his arms around her and hugged her close, careful not to crush the drawing paper that she still had a tight grip on. He was amazed that she had not dropped it.

"Nay, lass, I should be the one to apologize. I should not have done that. Not here, like this."

"It was, ah," she cleared her throat, "very nice."

The flush in her cheeks deepened, and he marveled at the fact that she was blushing.

"Ye liked it?"

"Aye," she whispered. "Very much."

Relief flooded through him, and he kissed her once more, a gentle graze of his lips across hers. "I promise to pay ye more mind in the future. Ye're my wife, and ye have my word that I'll make more time for ye… if that's what ye truly wish."

She smiled, and bent to place her sketches on the floor near her chair. Catriona pressed her hands against his chest and he could feel the heat of her through the front of his shirt. It was almost as warm as the wide smile she gave him.

"I would like that very much."

Liam took hold of her hands, keeping them pressed to his chest, and smiled. He could not remember the last time he felt so at peace.

"Ye should do that more often," Catriona told him.

"Do what?"

"Smile."

Liam chuckled, and nodded. "Aye. I suppose ye have not seen a great many of them from me, have ye?"

"No. But I'm looking forward to seeing more of them in the future." She sighed and looked around. "I love this room. I found it a few days ago, and have come here to draw every day since."

She bent down and picked up the sketches she had placed on the floor, offering them to him.

He studied her drawings, awed by how well she had captured the view from the window. The trees and lochs had such depth to them, it was a wonder that his hand did not sink into the page.

"These are wonderful."

"Ye're being kind."

"No. Ye're very talented. I'm glad that ye found a place in the keep where ye can draw." He paused and looked around the room, his mind flooded with the countless happy memories he had of it. "This was my mother's favorite place as well."

"Oh, Liam." She took his hand and squeezed it. "I am so sorry. I did not mean to intrude."

"Ye're not. I watched ye in here. Just for a moment, before ye noticed me. But even I could tell that ye belonged in here. My mother used to sit where ye are now, and stare out that window while she stitched. She loved to stitch…"

His eyes began to sting, and he turned his head away so that Catriona would not see the pain in his eyes.

"I am so sorry, Liam. Ye must miss her terribly. I was so young when I lost my mother that I barely remember her, and I still miss her terribly. I cannot imagine how much more painful it must be for you."

"Aye, it's painful. But I'm grateful for the time I had with her. With both my parents."

He stood up and looked out the window while continuing

to hold Catriona's hand. The words tumbled out of him, and he was unable to hold them back now that he had begun. "When I was very young, she would sit there and hold me on her lap. She would tell me stories and sing to me. Some of my happiest memories are in this room."

He looked down to see Catriona staring up at him with tears in her eyes. He reached over and brushed them away, touched that she would be so moved.

"I want ye to have this place now."

"Oh, Liam— " She began to protest but he cut her off.

"No. My mother would have wanted ye to have it and so do I. This room belongs to ye as it did to her. Make it yer own. Set up yer paints in here. It gets good light all year round. Ye need a place. Someplace that's just for you. I'd like for ye to have this one."

"I don't know what to say," she sniffed, wiping the tears from her eyes. "I would love to. Thank you so much."

Liam bent down and kissed her once more before releasing her hand.

"I have some things that need attending to, but I will see ye in the great hall for lunch."

"Are ye sure ye'll have time?"

He gazed down at her beautiful face, cursing himself for all the time he had wasted over the past week.

"Aye, wife. I'll have time."

CHAPTER 12

"SOMEONE FIND THE MACDONELL!" Frantic cries rang out across the courtyard.

The feeling of peace that had finally begun to settle in Liam for the first time since the wedding blew away like smoke at the urgent shouts that rang out for him.

Catriona hurried through the hallway behind him, trying to keep pace as he rushed to the entryway. The courtyard in front of the keep was a flurry of activity, and voices called out for the castle surgeon. He skidded to a stop at the sight of Alex being carried on a cot between four of his men. His blood ran cold.

"What happened?" Liam demanded as he rushed to his brother's side. The acid taste of fear rose in his throat as he gazed down upon his brother's pale face. Alex's eyes had been closed, but they fluttered open for a moment at the sound of his voice.

"Liam." Alex struggled to sit up but Liam restraint him.

"Hush now, Alex. Save yer strength."

Alex clutched his sleeve and tried to pull Liam closer with what little strength he still possessed. His pale blue eyes were glassy and wild as they bore into Liam before slipping away to look past him.

"'Tis the Drummonds," Alex hissed. "We heard their cry. We were outnumbered. They burned the houses to the ground, Liam. It was the Drummonds."

Alex collapsed. Liam turned slowly around to face where Alex had been staring. Catriona stood off to the side behind him, a mixture of fear and disbelief on her face.

The warmth they had begun to share turned to stone within him as he strode across the entry way toward her. He did not hesitate when the fear flashed across her face and she took a hasty step backward, but continued on until they were almost toe-to-toe.

Catriona had to tilt her head back in order to meet his gaze, but she stood her ground.

"Come with me." He barely recognized his own voice, it was so choked with fury. He grabbed Catriona roughly by the upper arm and dragged her out of the entryway and up to her bedchamber where he shoved her roughly inside and slammed the door behind them. He needed to speak with her, but wanted to do it away from the prying eyes of the keep. By now everyone downstairs would have heard Alex's accusations against Catriona's father. Keeping her locked upstairs was just as much for her own protection as it was necessary to hold her until he could find out what she knew about her father's deviousness.

Distrust and confusion raged within Liam as he paced back and forth in the chamber. He was unable to look at her, for fear that he would lose what precious little control he had on his temper. If Alex died, he would gather every man he had and raze Laird Drummond's lands to the ground. He would salt the earth so that the barren land would stand as a reminder to all others what would happen to those that would dare harm his family.

Liam's hands trembled with rage. He inhaled a ragged breath before coming to a halt and facing his wife. Her face looked almost as pale as his brother's had. She stood perfectly still, her eyes wide with fear as she took stock of him.

"Liam?" she whispered. "What has happened?"

He closed his eyes and turned his face away, searching for any whisper of trust that they had begun to build between them. He wanted to cling to it, unwilling to believe that he could have been so foolish as to allow himself to be taken in by a beautiful cunning viper for a second time. Was there no limit to a woman's deception?

"Your father…" He took a steadying breath and met her gaze once more. "Your father's men have been behind the reavings all along. Now they have burned my people's homes to the ground, attacked my brother's men, and have injured my brother. I do not know yet how badly."

Catriona's hands flew to her mouth, and she collapsed onto a nearby chair.

"No!" she shook her head in disbelieve. "No, that cannot be right. He would never… he *could* never! There must be some mistake. Some horrible, horrible mistake." Catriona refused to believe that her father was capable of ordering such brutality. He may have been a stubborn man, but he had never been cruel. An image flashed in her mind of how he had treated her the night he had caught her in Liam's chamber, but she quickly forced the thought away. That was completely different. He had only wanted what was best for her, and there was no sense in this.

"My brother saw them with his own eyes!" Liam shouted. "Heard their war cry! There was no mistake. Your father did this. I came to him for help, and he denied all of it. It was the perfect opportunity for him to wed me to one of his daughters. I knew he was behind it all. It was too convenient. And while he burns my clansmen's home to the ground I am wed to his daughter. I am twice the fool!"

"Ye cannot believe I had anything to do with this. Liam, please. I do not know why this is happening, but I promise ye it cannot be what it seems. My father would never do this!"

"And what do ye know of men and war, aye? What do ye know of how far a man is willing to go in order to get what it is he wants? Ye dinna think yer father is capable of such a thing? I'll tell ye now, lass, that yer father is capable of this and more. Of that I've nae doubt." He stalked towards her and clasped her chin gently in his trembling fingers. "But what about ye then? That is what I really want to know. What are ye capable of? Could ye have deceived me so completely over these past few days? Did ye know about yer father's plans all along?"

Catriona shoved his hand away from her face and glared up at him with fury in her eyes.

"The devil take ye, Liam MacDonell. I have had no part in the troubles that have plagued yer lands. I have not lied, or schemed, or done any of the other things ye are so keen to accuse me of. I dinna know what more I can do to prove to ye that ye can trust me. And no matter what ye think of my father, I can tell ye that he would never do such a thing. It makes no sense! I am his daughter and this is to be my home now. Why would he give the order to destroy it? Why would he do something that could put me in harm's way? Do ye really think that he would leave me here all alone and at yer mercy? Especially when it is so clear to see that ye have none!"

"I dinna ken. But rest assured that I will make him pay for what he has done."

Liam turned sharply on his heel and headed for the door.

"No!" Catriona shouted at his back. "Please, please dinna

do anything yet. Just let me speak to him. Let me find out the truth!"

"I suggest ye try to make yourself comfortable, wife of mine, because ye will not be going anywhere for a while."

Liam closed the door on her and locked it, trapping her inside.

He pushed back the wave of guilt that rose within him as the dull blows thudded on the door from where she pounded on it and shouted for him to release her. He did not want to hold her captive, but he could not risk her running off to her father while he tried to decide what do next.

But before he did anything, he needed to look in on Alex.

Liam's heart raced as he ran to Alex's bedchamber, heedless of those around him that pressed themselves up against the walls of the hallway in order to avoid getting knocked out of the way in his haste. By the time he burst through the doors of his brother's chamber, Iain was already there, sitting by their younger brother's side.

"How is he?"

Iain looked up, his face drawn, and shook his head as he clung to their brothers limp hand.

"Oh, God," Liam gasped stumbling forward. "Tell me he's not..."

"No," Iain reassured him. "He is only unconscious. But he has not spoken since they brought him here. They stitched his side where he was stabbed and set his arm. Both will heal in time, but he needs rest. Our brother is strong, he will make it through this, I know he will."

Liam lay a heavy hand on Iain's shoulder and squeezed it tightly.

"Drummond will not get away with this, I swear it to ye both."

Iain nodded before looking up at him. His eyes were a deep well of concern.

"Where is Catriona? I heard word that ye dragged her kicking and screaming up the stairs of the keep."

Liam shook his head. "Nothing so dramatic as that. Though she is locked in her chamber for the time being."

"Liam…" Iain frowned at him, disapproving.

"What would ye have had me do? Her father has brought naught but trouble upon us. Should I have just left her to run off to him?"

"She is yer wife."

"Perhaps, but until I can deal with her father and find out what part she played, if any, she is best left where she is for now. Besides, at the moment the keep is no safe place for her."

"She may not forgive ye for this Liam."

"I dinna need her forgiveness. What I need is her safety."

"And do ye really think that she will see it that way?"

"She'll come to understand in time. She won't have much choice about that."

"Liam, ye cannot force her to see yer way about things. I thought that the two of ye had begun to get along some?"

Liam let out a heavy sigh and sat down on a stood by Alex's bedside. "We had, at that. Sometimes, when I am with her and she smiles at me, I feel a calmness inside of me, a sense of peace that I have not felt in the longest time. But when I saw our brother lying there, bloody and bruised and accusing her kin, the feeling was gone and I dinna ken if it will ever return."

"Do ye still think that she had a hand in deceiving ye into marriage?"

"I'll tell ye Iain, I honestly dinna know. But I don't want to believe it."

"Then why are you so quick to make her pay for the choices her father has made? Catriona is not her father. She is yer wife. And locking her away is not going to make yer marriage any easier."

"I will fetch her when the time is right. But for now I stand by my decision. The keep is in an uproar. Ye may not know it, for ye've spent yer time down here with Alex, but people are cursing Drummond's name. I dinna want anyone to take their anger out on her. It's for her own safety that she simply stay out of sight for now until things calm down a bit."

"Are ye not worried that by locking her away ye may simply be finding the message to everyone that ye trust yer own wife even less than they do?"

Liam pinched the bridge of his nose and groaned. "I swear Iain, sometimes yer more annoying than a fly buzzing around my head. There are only so many battles that I can fight at once ye ken? Between Laird Drummond, Catriona, and worrying about Alex, I cannot also fight with you too."

Iain smiled and winked at him as he leaned back against the wall. "Well, ye wouldn't have to fight with me if ye simply listened to what I said every once in a while. It would make yer life much easier."

Liam snorted. "I doubt that very much."

Iain was silent a moment as he stared down at their brother's unconscious body. "Promise me that he'll be well."

Liam's jaw clenched and he jerked his head in a forceful nod. "Aye. He will. He has to be."

Iain nodded. "And if he's not?"

Liam looked his brother straight in the eye, his voice calm and unwavering. "Then I will take every single man that can be spared, ride to Laird Drummond's lands and burn every inch of it to the ground."

"Hmmm. How do ye think yer blushing bride will feel about ye burning down her family home?"

"If Alex dies, I really won't care."

CHAPTER 13

TIME CREPT by and Catriona's mind raced as she paced furiously back and forth in her bedchamber. Her hands were still sore from pounding her fists against the door, but it had been for naught. It was clear to her now that Liam had no intention of releasing her.

Devil take the man! His short temper would lead both of their people to utter ruin. Never in her life had she met anyone so untrusting. How could a man go through life forever fearful that those closest to him would do him some unforeseen slight? She had to find some way to reach her father before Liam started a war between the two clans.

If he wasn't so pigheaded, she was sure she would be able to convince him that there was no way her father could be behind any of this. But it was obvious that Liam was in no mood to listen to anyone, her least of all.

There was nothing for it then. She would simply have to find a way to get to the bottom of things on her own.

She looked around the room until her eyes landed on the dishes from her breakfast that had yet to be cleared away. She sent up a small prayer, thankful that she had slept late that morning and had decided to eat in her chamber. Rushing over to the table, she snatched up the knife with a sigh of relief. Throwing back the bed covers, Catriona went to work, using the knife to make a hole in the sheeting then tore it into long wide strips. Once she was finished she shoved the strips of cloth beneath the bed.

She lay down on the bed, heart racing, and prayed that her plan would work. Closing her eyes she took a deep breath and willed for sleep to come. She would need to be wide awake and well rested if she were to ride straight through the night.

Catriona was jerked out of an uneasy slumber by the sound of knocking at her door. Her body was heavy with exhaustion, protesting the rude awakening as she turned her head to see that the sun was almost set.

The lock turned in the door, spurring her to action, and she grabbed the knife which she had hidden under her bed and hurried to hide herself behind the chamber door. The sound of her heartbeat pounding in her ears was almost deafening, and she swiped her damp palms roughly over the skirt of her gown before retightening her grip on the knife hilt, fearful that it would slip from her unsteady hand.

"Begging yer pardon my lady, but I've brought ye some supper," said the young kitchen maid as she entered.

There was no time to doubt her plan. No time to think. If she did not move now her moment would be lost. Shoving aside her fear, Catriona stepped up behind the maid brought the knife up to the young girl's throat while kicking the bedchamber door closed with her foot.

The kitchen maid dropped the tray of food she was carrying and opened her mouth to scream as the plate and tray landed with a ringing clatter, but Catriona held her tight, and pressed the blade harder against her skin.

"Please, do not scream," she whispered.

The young woman closed her mouth and nodded slowly, but continued to whimper in fear.

"I'm sorry," Catriona told her. "I'm so very sorry, but Liam is making a terrible mistake and I have to get out of here so that I can stop it. Do ye understand?"

The girl nodded, her shoulders shaking as she sobbed silently.

"Good, that is good," said Catriona. She swallowed the bile that rose in her throat and fought the urge to be sick. Violence was not in her nature, but hundreds of lives were at risk, so she ignored the burning guilt the girl's tears evoked in her and she held her hand steady. If she showed any sign of physical weakness the girl could very well try to over-power her and escape.

"I feel terrible for what I am about to do, but I must tie ye up. I have to be sure that you will not alert anyone to my escape, do you see?"

Nudging the girl in the back, the two of them made their way slowly to the bed where Catriona motioned for her to sit on the floor.

"Now, slowly! Very slowly, raise your hands above your head. I am going to tie them to the post there."

"Please do not do this," the maid whispered, and hiccupped a sob.

"I have no choice," Catriona said apologetically. "I know you must be very scared. But please, if you just do what I say, everything will be all right."

Raising the maid's hands, Catriona tied her wrists tightly around the corner post of the bed and knotted it as soundly as she could before wrapping another strip of the torn sheet around the girl's waist.

"All right, and now your feet... Please," she told the girl.

"Must ye?" the girl sobbed.

"Begging me will do ye no good. I promise ye, I am doing

this for your own good as well as everyone else in this castle. What will happen to the people you care about if The MacDonell goes to war? I can stop it, I know I can."

Catriona held tightly to that belief as she struggled to block out the sound of the crying girl.

She tested the bindings and then, once satisfied, got to her feet.

"One last thing," she said and took a deep breath. "Open your mouth please."

"Wha—"

Moving quickly, she took advantage of the girl's confusion at Catriona's request, and she shoved a balled-up rag in her mouth. Then she grabbed the final strip of cloth, placed it over the girl's mouth, and secured it in a knot behind her head.

"I'm sorry, but I cannot have you calling for help. I have nae doubt that someone will come looking for you soon enough when you do not return to your duties. I just need a bit of a head start, that's all. Please forgive me."

Catriona flung her cloak over her shoulders and headed for the door but then stopped halfway there and turned back. A quick search of the girl's apron pockets revealed the chamber door key which she carried.

There was no turning back now. She stopped only for a moment to pick up the apple and piece of bread that had fallen to the floor when the girl had dropped the meal platter in surprise, then took a quick glance into the hall to make sure her way was clear before slipping outside. After shutting the door soundly behind her, she locked it, trapping the young maid securely inside.

Struggling to hold back her tears, she pressed her hand to the door, her heart going out to the scared girl. Then sent up a small prayer that her luck would continue to hold.

Hurrying as quietly as she could, Catriona rushed to the end of the hallway where she reached the staircase that led down to the main level of the keep.

She pulled the hood of her cloak over her head, kept her face low, and made her way down the stairs. The halls were empty as she hurried through them, and it suddenly struck her that the castle's inhabitants must all be in the great hall having their supper.

Not wanting to test her good fortune more than need be, she hurried out the front of the keep and across the empty yard until she reached the stables. Glancing around to make sure the stable hand wasn't inside, she walked past the occupied stalls until she spotted her mare in one of the far stalls.

"Hello there, girl," she said softly. The horse's mane was silky beneath her fingers and her bright white coat was glossy and soft. She was grateful to know that the stable boys had been taking such good care of her horse. Meera's eyes were bright and alert as she nudged her large head into Catriona's shoulder. "You're such a good horse, aren't you? Have you missed me?" Catriona cooed, holding up her hand for the horse to sniff.

Tossing her head, Meera stepped closer and nuzzled her nose into Catriona's neck. After a moment, Catriona placed a hand on the horses nose and stroked her gently. Meera had been her father's gift to her on her fifteenth birthday, and she had instantly fallen in love with the beautiful, gentle creature.

"Aren't you just lovely," she said. "You're so lovely, I've brought you a present." Catriona held the apple she had brought up in the air and watched as the horse eyed it in interest. "What do you think of the two of us going for a little ride? Would you like that?" The horse nipped the apple out of

Catriona's hand and she sighed in relief. It did not look as if the horse was going to make a fuss and bring anyone's attention's to the stable.

While the horse enjoyed its snack, Catriona found a blanket, saddle and bridle, and wasted no time in saddling the horse, grateful that she had paid attention to the lessons her father's stable master had taught her growing up. Knowing how to saddle her own horse on her own had always been a boon when she wanted to sneak away from home to go out painting.

Once Meera was saddled and she was ready to go, Catriona grabbed a horseshoe hanging from the wall. She checked to make sure everyone was still inside before leading the horse away from the stables.

There was only one guard at the gate. The other had most likely gone to the hall to bring them both back their meals, which meant he would not be gone for long. Before the guard was alerted to her presence, Catriona sneaked up behind him and struck him with the iron horseshoe across the back of the head.

The guard let out a grunt and crumbled to the ground in a heap. Catriona let out a whimper at the sight of blood on the back of the unconscious man's head, but would not allow herself to fall into despair. Liam would be furious when he saw what she had done, but so long as she could bring back proof that some other treachery was at hand and clear her father's name, maybe her husband would be inclined to forgive her.

Catriona mounted the mare and fled the castle, pushing the horse as hard as she could. Every minute counted in putting as much distance between her and the men who were sure to follow. The horse thundered down the long stretch of road until they came upon a fork in the road. One way led directly to her father's land, the other would get her there eventually, but was a more indirect route.

She looked back and forth between the two paths. She needed to make it to Drummond land as soon as she could, but Liam and his men would surely expect her to take the more direct route. She may not get back to her father's lands as quickly, but taking the longer road may just give her the advantage she needed.

Making her choice, Catriona guided the horse to the left and down the road that cut through the woods.

Catriona rode for hours following the winding path through the trees. The sun had long since set, and the moon, not even half full, barely helped to guide her way through the dense overhang of the forest. She wrapped her cloak more tightly around her shoulders to warm her against the night's chill and tried to stay focused on the task ahead. But with every step her horse took it felt as though the trees were closing in around her, and she could not escape the feeling that someone or something was watching her from the trees.

"Dinna be ridiculous," she scolded herself. "There is absolutely nothing out there."

A wolf's howl went up and the mare reared wildly, almost bucking her off. Catriona scrambled to hold tightly to the reins and tried to bring Meera under control, but when the second wolf howl went up in the night the horse took off thundering down the road and it was all Catriona could do to stay in the saddle.

"Easy there, girl!" Catriona shouted as she pulled back on the reins. But Meera continued to gallop at full speed as though she could feel the hot breath of the wolves snapping at her heels.

Catriona continued to struggle with the reins until finally the horse began to slow. Once she was back under control,

Catriona guided her to a full stop to give herself a moment to settle her nerves. In truth, she had been more terrified of the prospect of losing her seat and breaking her neck in the fall than the idea that there were wolves somewhere around them in the trees. She climbed down off the horse and took a deep breath to steady herself. Her knees were weak, but she was in desperate need of feeling solid ground beneath her feet.

"Well now," said a voice in the darkness, causing her to jump and shriek in terror.

Catriona spun around to see a man emerge from the tree line.

"The two of ye made enough noise thundering down the road to wake the dead. Are ye in need of help, lass?"

Catriona moved closer to her horse, still unable to make out the man's features in the darkness.

"No, thank you. If you will excuse me, I need to be on my way."

"Now what kind of man would I be if I let a bonny lass like ye wander around by yerself in the woods? Come warm yerself by the fire."

"Thank you, but no—" A hand landed on Catriona's shoulder from behind and she broke off in a started shriek.

"Please, we insist," a deep voice said in her ear.

CHAPTER 14

"Catriona?" Liam knocked on the door of his wife's bedchamber but there was no answer. He had no doubt that she was sulking. Women always used silence as a punishment.

Why in Heaven had he allowed Iain to convince him to come upstairs and check on her? He was the last person she would want to see.

He knocked on the door again, harder this time. "Catriona, are you awake?"

He heard a soft thumping noise coming from inside the chamber and frowned. What the devil was she doing in there? Looking for something heavy to brain him with, no doubt. Liam unlocked the door and entered the dark chamber. There was not a single candle lit in the room. But the dim light of the moon illuminated the bulk of a person on the floor near the bed with their arms suspended above their head.

"Catriona!" He rushed over to untie her. But when he bent down and looked into her face he saw that it was not Catriona at all, but Mary, one of the kitchen maids.

"What the devil is going on here?" he demanded.

Mary tried to speak from behind her gag, but she could not form any words and began crying in frustration.

"Hush now, Mary, give me a moment," He spoke gently and kept his voice low, hoping to keep her calm while he removed the binding from her mouth.

"Oh thank ye. Thank ye, Laird MacDonell. I dinna know what I would have done if ye had not come along."

"What happened here?" he asked as he went to work on the bindings around her ankles and then stood to make quick work of the ones around her wrists. "Who did this to ye, lass?"

"It was Lady Catriona," the girl said with a sob as she rubbed her tender wrists.

"What!?" Liam exploded.

"It was yer new wife, sir. I came to bring the Lady Catriona her supper hours and hours ago. But when I entered she held a knife to my throat and bound me to the bed, then made her escape. I'm so sorry, Laird MacDonell, I was so scared. I could do nothing to stop her!"

Liam heard the maid's words, but he could make no sense of them. While he and Catriona had not been married long, there had been no sign of a violent nature in her. But perhaps she truly was as treacherous as he had feared after all.

"Come lass, we had best get ye seen to. Then I will find Catriona and make her answer for this."

"Oh no, Laird MacDonell, there's no time. Ye must know. The Lady mentioned that she was going back to her father. There is no telling how far from the castle she is now."

"Gone to rejoice with him in a plan well executed, no doubt," he spat. Rage and betrayal welled up inside of him, spreading like a poison. That was what he got for thinking there might be a single woman to walk the earth who wouldn't lead a man to pain and ruin.

"I dinna know about all of that." She sniffled and wiped the tears from her eyes. "There was no joy in her. She said that she was tying me up for my own good. Mine and all of your people. And that she had to stop ye from making a terrible mistake. I was scared out of my wits and nae doubt, but... tis the strangest thing. I swear to ye she was doing it to help ye."

"Ye've had a terrible time of it, I know. Dinna think on it anymore," he said, wanting to dismiss what she had said. But her words continued to plague him as he led her gently to the door.

"She apologized to ye? Truly?" he asked hesitantly.

"Aye, she did. She fair begged me to understand why she would do such a thing. I dinna know what it is that may be going on between you and her father, and it is not my business. I know that I'm speaking well above myself to even mention it, and I would not even dare to do such a thing, if it were not for the fact that she mentioned *war*, Laird MacDonell." The maid turned to look up at him with kindness in her eyes. "And I can understand that ye see. I can understand why a good person may feel they need to do a bad thing if it means they can stop an even worse thing from happening."

"Ye have a very forgiving heart, lass," he told her. "There are not many who would be able to forgive such a slight against them." Looking down at Mary, he saw that even though she had spent the last few hours bound, alone and in the dark, there was, to his great surprise, no anger or malice in her eyes. She obviously believed what she had said to be true. Had Catriona truly been so convincing that she had been able to earn the poor lass's forgiveness for the crimes done against her?

Did Catriona truly believe that she was doing the right thing? And would she go to lengths such as this? She should have waited for him to come to her, so that she could tell him whatever it was she needed to say, not attack innocent young women.

Now she was out there on the road. In the dark, where anything could happen to her. Even as he cursed her foolishness, he could not quell the nagging voice in his head that said this entire situation was his fault. Why would she speak to him? He had showed her that afternoon that he cared not for what she had to say. He had locked his new wife away like a criminal and left her trapped in her chamber for hours on end, all because he was unable to control his temper.

Liam brushed the irritating thoughts aside. None of that mattered now. What mattered was that Catriona had at least five hours' head start on him, and he had to move quickly if he was going to catch up with her in the dark. When he found her, he promised himself that he would listen to what she had to say with an open mind. If he didn't break her lovely headstrong neck first.

CHAPTER 15

CATRIONA KICKED and struggled against her captors as the two men hauled her through the trees. Bright sparks rose from a small fire pit around which five other men sat huddled, talking and laughing boisterously.

"Look what we found on our rounds, lads," said the man who had come up behind her out of nowhere. "Is she not a lovely wee thing?"

Catriona gasped as she was suddenly released and thrown roughly down onto the cold hard ground at the men's feet.

One of the men leaned down and grabbed her chin roughly with dirt-stained fingers and raised her head. His lips were dry and cracked, and he had a few days' worth of hair on his jaw. Catriona squeezed her eyes shut and tried to turn her face away, but he tightened his grip. The foul odor of his breath invaded her nose. It was pungent and sour with the smell of onions on top of it. He leaned in closer to look at her and for one terrifying moment Catriona feared that he would attempt to kiss her, but suddenly the pressure was gone from her jaw and she was released.

Panting heavily, she looked around the circle of men with

a glare and struggled to her feet. Over the last two weeks she had been attacked by a drunkard, forced to marry a man who despised her, was locked in her own bedchamber, and was now lost in the forest and attacked by men once more. Catriona was at the end of her patience. She had had more than enough of male brutes and their high-handed treatment of her. Strangers, her husband, and even her own father treated her as though she were little more than a plaything for their own gain and amusement. Well, she was having none of it. Not anymore.

"I demand that you release me this instant. How dare you treat me in this manner."

"A bit high handed for a harlot, is she not?" said one of the men.

Catriona rounded on him, outraged. "How dare you? I am not a harlot!"

Sharp, jagged fingernails dug into her arm, and she winced in pain as she was jerked around forcibly, her body twisted uncomfortably while her knees slid across the rocky ground. Catriona's heart quickened in fear at the sight of this man. The light of the fire illuminated the hard line of his mouth and the crags of his face. There was a long, raised red scar down the side of his face. It looked as though whoever had attacked him had just barely missed blinding the man. Catriona did not doubt that whoever had done it was now surely dead. Because it was not the scar or look of him that scared her so. No, it was his eyes. They were such a dark brown they looked to be black, and in them she saw no life, nor feeling, nor mercy. There was nothing but an empty void filled with icy cold that made Catriona want to shiver at his touch, no matter how close she was standing to the warmth of the fire.

"Not a whore, ye say," he spoke softly, but it only made his deep voice all the more menacing. Catriona could see a barely restrained rage in the man, and she had no doubt he would not hesitate to do her violence. "What kind of woman but a whore would be riding through the woods unaccompanied in the middle of the night?"

Catriona trembled, and continued to stare into his eyes, trapped in his gaze, fearing that if she were to look away, even for a single moment, he would strike out like a snake.

"A desperate woman," she whispered.

"Desperate, aye," he nodded and examined her face slowly. His eyes traveled over every inch of it as though he could read every secret she ever held as clearly as if it were written on her skin in ink. "And what is yer name, my wee desperate lass."

"I am Catriona Drummond, daughter of Laird Ewan Drummond, Chief of Clan Drummond," she told him. "I am trying to get home to my father. If ye take me to him unharmed, ye will be well rewarded for it. I swear."

"Reward us, will he?" His smile chilled Catriona to the bone. "Well, I suppose we could consider it. Though I dinna doubt that my men might consider ye a reward in itself." He trailed a finger slowly down her cheek, and Catriona's stomach rolled in revulsion.

"If you do anything to harm me, I swear my father will not stop until he has hunted you all down and gutted ye like cattle. That is not a threat, it is the plain truth of it. So please, either release me or help me reach him." Catriona held her breath, waiting to see how he would react. She worried that she may have pushed too far. But she would rather tell them the truth of who she was and be bartered for ransom than be victim to their whims. And since news of her marriage to Laird MacDonell had not spread yet there was no way for them to know that her husband was the one they should truly be trying returning her to. Maybe all was not yet lost.

The cold-eyed man laughed and released her. Catriona

gave a sigh of relief when he turned away from her, until she heard his command:

"Tie her up."

"What? No! I will not run, just take me back to my father. Please, I beg ye!" She was grabbed roughly from behind once more, and soon she felt the rough slide of rope along her wrists.

"And gag her," the man added. "I dinna want to have to listen to her bleat on all night."

Catriona's curses were muffled behind the gag in her mouth as two of the men dragged her to a nearby tree and tied her to it.

"There, now," one of them said as he finished tying the rope. "Dinna go making any trouble, and ye might still make it out of this with all of your teeth in yer mouth. Ye dinna want to go making that one angry." He gave the rope a tug to test the bonds and nodded, satisfied with his work. Catriona glared at his back as he walked away from her to go enjoy sitting next to the warmth of the fire.

When she glanced away she noticed that one of the other men was staring at her, but when her gaze caught his, he quickly looked away. His shoulders were hunched over and the bulk of his body was turned away from her, showing him to be narrow of build. He had wrapped a length of his plaid around his shoulders, and looked to be trying to tuck it up around his ears in an attempt to obscure his face. Catriona sat there watching him, and every few minutes, the man's eyes darted back in her direction again for only a moment before once more looking away.

Catriona studied him silently. There was something about him that felt familiar, but she could not place where she knew the man from.

She shivered and tried to adjust herself into a more

comfortable position but it did not work, the ropes were much too tight.

"So," she heard one of the men say, "what are we going to do with her then?"

"We should take her back to Laird Drummond. He would pay a pretty price to have her back," said another.

Catriona stopped fidgeting and held herself still in order to hear their conversation more clearly.

"We will not be taking her back to Laird Drummond," said the cold-eyed man. He walked around the fire, circling the men. "I have a better idea. A much more profitable one."

There was some grumbling, but none of the others outright challenged him. Whoever he was, the men were obviously afraid of him.

"Ye'll have us all dancin' at the end of a rope," came a muffled slurred voice.

The cold-eyed man stopped and turned to face the man who had spoken.

"Do ye have a better plan, then, Angus?"

The man, who Catriona assumed was Angus, stood up and swayed on his feet, standing toe-to-toe with the leader.

"I said, ye'll have us all dancin' at the end of a rope. Ye'll be the death of us all. MacDonell will see us all dead if he finds us on his lands after what we did to that family. And now we have Drummond's daughter. The ransom we could get for her would be enough to put us safely out of The MacDonell's reach. We could deliver her in two, maybe three days, and ye dinna want to do it?" Angus looked around at the others in disgust. "When I was the leader, did I not make sure ye lads were paid? Did I not make sure ye were safe? And then one day ye," he whirled on the other man and jabbed a finger roughly into his chest, "just decided ye would take over. Claiming to have a whole second set of orders. Ye could have forged that letter for all we know. The whole thing is insanity! We should take the girl back to her father. It's Drummond's fault we're in this mess anyway. Him and that old bastard Macnaghten—"

The cold-eyed man moved quickly, pulled out his knife, and stabbed Angus in the gut with it before he could finish what he was going to say. Angus clutched his stomach with a look of surprise.

"Wha—" he choked out, but Catriona did not get to hear what Angus was going to say next because the cold-eyed man brought the knife up and across Angus's throat.

She watched in horror as Angus tried to clutch at both his stomach and throat in turn as he fell to his knees and then collapsed face down in the dirt.

"We will not be taking her back to Laird Drummond," the cold eye man said. His voice was still light, but there was no mistaking the steel behind it. "Is that clear?"

The men nodded their heads and mumbled their assent.

"Good. We set out at first light tomorrow. There is someone she will be much more valuable to than her father."

Catriona sat shivering as hot tears rolled down her cheeks as she stared at Angus's dead body lying on the ground. Not a single man moved to bury him. They simply left him where he lay.

She closed her eyes, trying to block out the sight, but in the darkness behind her eyes, all she could see was the look of surprise on his face when he realized that he had been stabbed, and hear him say over and over again in her mind, "It's Drummond's fault we're in this mess anyway."

"Wake up,"

Catriona was jerked awake by the toe of a hard boot being shoved into her tender side. She had been tied to a tree all night, and her arms, legs, and backside were all feeling incredibly numb. She couldn't help but wonder if this was her payment for what she had done to the kitchen maid in order to make her escape. Catriona hoped that the girl had been found before too long. Her stomach twisted with guilt and worry at the thought of the young girl, trapped in Catriona's bedchamber all night, but someone must have gone in search of her once she had been away from the kitchen for too long.

Catriona winced as she was jabbed in the side again, this time more sharply. She tried to ignore the boot and kept her eyes closed in a weak attempt to welcome back the oblivion that sleep allowed.

"I said, wake up!" There was another, harder kick to the side, one that she could not ignore, and Catriona cried out in pain.

"Enough!" she snapped. "I am awake."

"It's time for us to head out. If ye give me any problems when I untie ye, ye'll taste the back of my hand, understood?"

Catriona nodded and sat still while the man untied the ropes that bound her to the tree. The man took her by her arm and hauled her to her feet. Her knees felt week and a sharp tingling pain shot through her limbs as the blood flow returned to them.

"Come on, then," he said.

"I... cannot go yet," Catriona said, her face flushing with embarrassment.

"I dinna remember asking ye for your opinion on the matter."

"I must... I must relieve myself," she whispered.

The man glared at her and waited.

"Well I cannot do it here! All I am asking for is a bit of privacy," she told him.

"Well, ye will not be going by yourself."

Catriona's face was flaming but she did not argue with the man. She knew it would do her no good. But there was no way she would relieve herself in the view of the entire group of men.

"Can I ye not at least accompany somewhere a bit more secluded?"

The man sighed in annoyance and tugged her roughly off towards a patch of bushes.

"And where do ye think ye're headed off to with the lass, eh?" one of the other men called.

"Our Lady Drummond here needs to take a piss!" her escort called back loudly.

Catriona wished for the ground to open up and swallow her. She thought that she would die of embarrassment. The raucous waves of laughter assaulted her back as she hurried to position herself behind the bush.

She bent over to gather up her gown but when she looked up she saw that the man was watching her, and she froze.

"Ye cannot possibly expect me to do this with ye watching me?" she snapped.

"Boss said that I'm not to take my eyes off of ye or else I'll end up as dead as auld Angus over there." He jerked his thumb over his shoulder to where Angus still lay cold in the dirt.

Catriona turned her head away in shame and tried to concentrate on the job at hand. It was not easy, but eventually she was able to block out the feeling of the man's eyes on her while she relieved herself.

As he led her back to the group, she saw that their small camp was already stripped down and the men were ready to move. They were taking her mare with them, so at least she would have her own horse to ride.

Catriona moved towards where the mare she had

borrowed from MacDonell was grazing nearby, but a large chest suddenly stepped into her path and blocked her way.

Catriona stopped in her tracks as fear rolled over her. She did not need to look up into his face to know who it was. There was only one man whose presence terrified her so.

"Ye'll be riding with me," he told her.

He did not touch her, or force her to follow him. He simple turned on his heel and made his way over to a large grey stallion without a single glance back, certain that she would follow.

Catriona was no fool. Though everything in her tried to convince her that this was her chance to flee, she knew it to be folly. She would never make it to her horse. She would not make it more than two steps in the opposite direction before his men would be on her. And she had no doubt that the punishment for her disobedience would be severe.

So Catriona followed him silently as her hatred for the man simmered within her.

"Get up," he ordered, pointing to the horse.

Catriona scrambled up into the saddle and took hold of the reins. Her hands tightened around them as the taste of freedom surged through her, and then a heavy hand suddenly landed on her thigh, squeezing it tightly.

"I would not try it if I were ye, lass. He will not take off without me, so ye had best be putting any thought of escape out of yer mind, unless ye are wanting me to walk behind the horse for the entire journey instead of ride upon him?"

Catriona shook her head no, and held herself very still as he climbed upon the horse behind her. His arms came around her to take the reins and she leaned forward slightly, wanting to put some distance between their two bodies. Her skin crawled at the intimate nature of their riding together. The cold detachment Liam had showed her on their journey to Invergarry was now almost a fond memory.

It did not take long, however, for Catriona to become incredibly uncomfortable holding herself in the saddle in such an unnatural position, and eventually she had to give in and rest her back against his chest. Even that light contact between them turned the blood to ice in her veins.

The men rode in silence as they continued down the forest road. They did not talk or laugh or joke, merely followed behind their leader without even the knowledge of where he was taking them.

When they rounded a bend in the road, Catriona looked back at the other riders and her eyes collided with a familiar face. She recognized the narrow build and hunched set of his shoulders from the night before, but now in the bright light of day she finally understood why he had tried to conceal himself from her.

It was the man who had attacked her in the hallway the night her father had forced her to marry Liam MacDonell.

CHAPTER 16

CATRIONA WRAPPED her arms around herself and shivered within the many folds of the belted earasaid that she had wrapped tightly around her shoulders.

It was late afternoon on the fourth day of their journey, and it had been raining for the past two days. Catriona could not believe her ears when, instead of stopping to look for shelter, her captor had ordered their small group to ride on.

Her skirts clung heavily to her legs, and her hair lay in thick matted locks that had plastered themselves to the side of her face. She was soaked to the skin and every last inch of her was bone cold.

Because of the direction they had ridden in from when they had first captured her, Catriona knew that they must have passed through Drummond land, but they had not gone anywhere near the castle, keeping her well away from her father.

Catriona cast her gaze over to the narrow, hunched man who rode with them. Every so often she could feel his gaze upon her. She tried to ignore his furtive glances, feigning ignorance of her realization of who the man was. But inside, her mind was racing. He was not one of her father's men, that much was clear. Neither was he one of Liam's. So how was it that he had been there to attack her beneath her father's very roof? It was very unlikely that he would have been invited as one of the wedding guests, so the question was, what had the loathsome man been doing there in the first place?

She had had four days of silence. Her days were spent on horseback, with the cold-eyed man ever near. Her nights were spent with her wrists and ankles bound, tied to the nearest tree, her every movement watched to ensure she did not try to flee. Four long, hard days of not knowing her fate. And in that entire time, not once had any of the men spoken their leader's name. She had only ever heard the man be referred to as 'he' or 'him' but nothing more.

It were as though to utter his name was to enchant some kind of dark curse. As though they feared it would call him forth, drawing his attention, and he would look into them with those cold, empty eyes of his before dragging them back down to the pits from whence he came.

These men had no love for him, only fear. But what power could he possibly possess that would compel them all to stay despite how they felt about him? Who *was* he? And what were his plans for her? Catriona was still nowhere nearer to knowing what was to happen to her once they reached their destination.

Angus's final words continued to plague her. She tried to quell her nausea at the memory of how he died and focused on what he had been saying just before it happened. What mess were the men in and what did her father have to do with it? They had mentioned a fire and The MacDonell's anger. She had a sneaking suspicion that these were the men Liam's brother Alex had attempted to hunt down and bring to justice. The ones Liam had accused of being under her father's orders.

She still did not want to believe it. From what she had seen, her da had always been a kind and just man. So what business did he have dealing with men such as these? She refused to accept that he would ever have anything to do with this group of thieves and murderers.

As they trudged on, the sky turned dark and angry. The rain poured down on them in sheets and the wind whipped around them. A bright fork of lighting cracked across the sky, followed closely by a deep roll of thunder, and the horses went wild. Neither man nor beast wanted to be out in such hellish weather.

A loud neigh rang out, and Catriona turned to see Meera rear up before landing heavily and kicking out with her back legs. They had not allowed her to ride her mare, to ensure she would not be able to flee. The man holding Meera's reins lost his grip on her, and a moment later the horse was free. Meera wasted no time in turning around and thundering down the road, back the way they had come.

"Get that horse!" the dark-eyed man yelled before anyone could go after her. "We are almost there."

Even though fear for her own situation gripped Catriona, she could not help but feel happy for the mare that had gotten free. With any luck they would not catch her, and the horse would make her way back home to the stables at Drummond Castle. She hated the idea of such a gentle animal being pressed into service at the mercy of these men.

As they rode on, two of the riders broke away from the group to chase down her horse.

They rode on a few hours more, and Catriona heaved a sigh of relief as they made their way through the gates of a castle she had never before visited. While she was fearful of what was to become of her now that they had reached their destination, she was grateful to soon be getting off of the horse and out of the cold rain.

The keep was small compared to her father's sprawling estate, but roughly the same size as Invergarry. And though it may have just been the effect of the terrible weather on her mood, there was something rather eerie about the place. Catriona looked up at the dark face of the castle and felt unsettled.

Her captor climbed down from the horse and waited for Catriona to follow, but her legs were tangled in her heavy, sopping-wet skirts, and she struggled to swing her leg over to dismount.

Grabbing her about the waist, the black-eyed man hauled her off of the animal and deposited her onto the ground in one smooth move. It brought her mind back to her arrival at Liam's home. But this time, the touch of strong hands around her waist did not fill her with surprising feelings of warmth and longing. Instead there was only dread at what was to come.

She was led to the large entry where the black-eyed man pounded heavily on the door. The small group of men huddled together in a tight group, all eager to get inside out of the storm.

The leader pounded again, and the door was soon opened, by a short timid young girl. She could have been no more than twelve.

"Aye, sir?" she asked. Her voice was so quiet, Catriona was barely able to hear her over the howling wind.

"Tell Macnaghten that he has guests," the black-eyed man told her as he shoved past the girl into the hall. "And tell him that I have something he is going to want very much."

Catriona stood just inside the doorway of the keep, shivering so hard that her teeth rattled from the tremors as her soaked clothing dripped onto the floor in the entryway.

"What in blazes is this?"

Catriona turned in the direction of the raised voice to see a short portly man come barreling toward them with a thunderous expression on his face.

"What are ye and yer men doing here? And who the devil is she?"

"Laird Macnaghten," the dark-eyed man said. "I've brought ye a gift. May I introduce ye to Catriona Drummond, youngest daughter of Laird Ewan Drummond."

At the sound of her name Laird Macnaghten's face faded from bright red to deathly pale, and his hands curled into tight fists at his sides.

"What is she doing here?" he asked in a strangled voice.

"I thought ye might find some use for her."

Macnaghten shot a withering stare at her captor.

"Ye blundering, half-witted fool!" he shouted. "Ye risk bringing her here on a damned whim? Take her, quickly before anyone sees!"

Catriona let out a cry as she was suddenly grabbed by many hands, including one firm hand that was placed over her mouth.

Laird Macnaghten stepped forward until he was toe-to-toe with the black-eyed man. The fact that the Laird was a good few inches shorter seemed to make no difference. He looked at Catriona's captor at though he were no more significant than the muck on the bottom of the Laird's shoe, with none of the fear that she nor the other men had of the group's leader.

"I should have ye whipped for this Gavin, and if ye dinna watch yerself, I still might. Now bring her." He turned sharply and led them into the keep. "I need some time to sort out how to best deal with yer mess."

Gavin grabbed Catriona roughly by the arm and yanked her out of the grips of the other men.

"Wait for me here," he snapped at them, before following behind Macnaghten.

So the devil had a name after all.

Catriona glanced at the man Macnaghten had called Gavin out of the corner of her eye. How odd it was to now have a name for him, and one that made him seem all too human at that. With eyes as cold and as black as his, he had seemed more creature than man on their journey. It was strange seeing him take orders from anyone, even a Laird. Out in the great expanse of the woods and the darkness of the night, he had seemed to her almost a demon. But now he had a name, and a master whom he obeyed, and seeing these things bolstered Catriona's confidence. Black eyes or no, Gavin was a man like any other. And from what she could tell, he had made a grave mistake in bringing her here.

She eyed Macnaghten's back as she was whisked down the hall. This man knew her father, she was certain of it, but was that something she could use to convince him to let her go? He obviously did not want her here. Maybe all hope was not lost after all.

CHAPTER 17

LIAM HAD RIDDEN out into the night alone as fast as his horse would take him. He had hoped to overtake Catriona on the road before she was able to reach the safety of her father's home, but somehow he had not caught so much of a glimpse of her.

Wind and rain lashed at his face, but he continued on. He had already lost a day of travel due to the storm. The winds had been too strong, and the roads too treacherous to travel safely, so he had been forced to take shelter until the storm had eased some. By the time he reached Drummond Castle, his ire had built to the point of boiling over. Four days gone now, and he had no way of knowing how his brother fared, or if young Alex was even still alive. If his brother did not make a full and speedy recovery, Drummond would be sure to pay for it with his life.

He galloped up the long road that passed through the expansive grounds that Drummond Castle sat upon and up to the front of the manor house, receiving no more than a passing nod and curious glances from the men standing guard.

"I'm here to speak with Laird Drummond," he called over the howling of the wind.

One of the men nodded and beckoned Liam to follow him into the mansion.

Maybe Catriona had not yet made it back. It was the only thing that would explain why his arrival was met with no resistance. It was possible that the storm had been too much for her to ride through on her own, and she was still sheltered somewhere waiting for it to pass so that she could continue on her travels safely.

Liam had been battered by rain, but he paid his soaking-wet clothes no mind, even as he left great puddles in his wake while making his way through the mansion until he was led to Laird Drummond's library.

Laird Drummond's clansman knocked lightly on the door and waited patiently until they finally heard Drummond's voice call, "Enter," from the other side of the door.

The clansman opened the door to show Liam inside.

"Laird MacDonell to see ye, Laird Drummond."

Laird Drummond gave a nod, and with that, his guide took his leave.

"Where is she?" Liam demanded as way of greeting as he stormed into Drummond's library. "Where is that treacherous daughter of yers I must now call 'wife'?"

Drummond sat back in his chair and rested his folded hands on his stomach.

"Lost her already, have ye? Well, now, that was rather careless," the older man boomed.

"Ye think this is a joke, Drummond? Ye force me to marry yer daughter, and ye set men to destroy my land. To kill my people! Is it war ye're after? Because I'd be more than happy to oblige ye!" Liam laid a hand on the hilt of his sword, and he heard a sharp intake of breath come from the corner of the large room.

Liam whirled round to discover that the two men were not alone as he had first assumed, but in fact, Laird Drummond's two other daughters had been reading quietly in the corner the entire time.

Their books fell to their laps, forgotten, and they stared at him with mingled expressions of shock, confusion, and fear on their faces.

"Those are some very serious accusations ye've laid against me, lad," Laird Drummond said, sitting up straight in his chair and placing his clasped hands on the ornately carved wood desk in front of him. Do ye have any proof of these things?"

"Proof?" Liam spat.

"Aye, proof. Ye come in here, shouting about war with yer hand on yer hilt and yer head so far up yer own arse it's a wonder ye made it to my door at all without getting lost on the road out there. So I ask ye, Liam MacDonell, what proof do ye have for these things ye accuse me of?"

Liam stared the man down, and his rage grew as he realized that Drummond was right. While every bone in his body told him that the man was behind it, he had no hard evidence to lay at the man's feet.

"'Tis all too convenient," he said finally. "The growing thefts on my land forced me to come to ye for help, and when I turned down your demands to marry one of yer daughters, I somehow found myself forced into it anyway mere hours later. And now these reavers have burned down houses and set upon my youngest brother. He barely made it back to us alive. And if that is not damning enough, Catriona has now run off, to come back here and warn ye, no doubt, that I was on my way here to see justice done."

Laird Drummond had listened to Liam's tirade with an expression of little more than mild annoyance until the second mention of his daughter, when the man suddenly went very pale as all the blood drained from his face.

"Catriona has run off?" Laird Drummond asked, "Truly?"

"Aye, and I was only a few hours behind her but did not overtake her on the road." He saw the concern on Drummond's face, and released the hilt of his sword and relaxed his stance. The man look truly concerned.

"Did she not make it back here?" he asked, suddenly feeling a concern of his own. Whether Catriona had betrayed him or not, he did not like the idea of her being lost outside in that storm.

"I swear I have not seen or spoken to my daughter since the morning after the two of ye were wed."

"What about your other daughters?" Liam asked, turning to the two young women. "Have either of ye seen Catriona?"

The girls shook their heads no, and a tight burning knot of fear began to grow in Liam's stomach.

"Speak up!" Laird Drummond roared, surging to his feet. "If ye've heard from yer sister, ye will tell me now and tell me true. I don't care where ye may have hidden the lass away, so long as ye tell me where she is at once!"

His two daughters jumped in fright and stared wide-eyed at their father.

"We have not seen her," the eldest said firmly, holding her father's gaze. "We are not hiding her anywhere."

Brigid, Laird Drummond's redheaded daughter's gaze flickered to Liam's for the briefest of moments before replying, "I have not seen her, da, I swear it. Neither of us have."

"Blast and damnation!" Laird Drummond circled around the tables and headed for the library door. "Aileen, come with me. We must form a search party to find yer sister. Help me rouse the men. I'll not have my daughter cold and out alone on this godforsaken night. Hurry up, lass!"

Laird Drummond barreled past Liam and was out the door before he even had a chance to speak.

Brigid followed after her sister, but at the last moment Liam reached out quickly and grabbed her firmly by the upper arm.

"What are ye not telling me, lass?" he asked quietly.

Brigid narrowed her eyes and regarded him coolly.

"I dinna know what ye mean. Now kindly unhand me," she told him, and tried to tug her arm out of his grip, but Liam would not release her.

"I know that ye're hiding something, so spit it out and be quick about it. Yer sister could die out in a storm like this, or the men that go to find her could be injured. Is that what ye want if she is not even actually out there? To send yer father's men on a pointless search on such a hellish night?"

Brigid considered him for a moment before jerking her head toward the door. "Make sure they are both gone," she told him.

Liam hesitated then slowly released her and went to check outside the door.

"We are alone," he told her. "Now what do ye know?"

"I dinna know where my sister is, I dinna lie about that. I swear it. I just... I was not sure if I should tell ye what I *do* know."

Liam wanted to strangle the girl for wasting time playing games.

"I suggest ye speak up and tell me before I lose what little patience I have left with yer scheming family."

Brigid took a step toward him with her hands clenched into tight shaking fists at her side. Her pale face was bright red in anger, complimenting her deep flaming auburn hair.

"Did it ever occur to ye that Catriona may be just as unhappy about the situation as ye obviously are?" she demanded.

"Is that so?" he snorted. Catriona may not have been thrilled at the thought of being married to him, but it was highly unlikely that she could be as unhappy about it as he was, especially now in the light of her father's obvious treachery. He had believed that she wanted them to find happiness. But perhaps acting had been her true talent, and not painting after all.

"She told us, ye ken? The truth of what happened to her. That she was attacked by some flea-ridden drunkard in the hall, and that ye sheltered her until she felt safe enough to leave. She thought ye her hero. I could see it in her face, the way she spoke of ye. My sister is gentle and kind. Much more gentle and kind than I've ever been," she said with a light snorting laugh. "She was so horrified to have put ye in the position of having to wed her, yer only crime being nothing more than showing her kindness. She told us that she begged our da to see reason, but he would not. She was forbidden to speak the truth to anyone."

Brigid glared at Liam with disgust and hatred burning in her eyes. "We cannot even find the man that truly meant her harm and bring him to justice, because that would be admitting that our father played ye false as a means to his own ends. All Cat wanted to do was be a good wife to ye, to show ye that even though ye didn't want to wed her, ye would not spend the rest of yer days regretting it. And now here ye are. Barging into our home with threats of war and unfounded accusations. Is this what ye have shown my sister in the short time she was with ye? This hatred and distrust? This disgust for her?" she spat. "And ye wonder why she would run from ye? Why she would seek out her family to protect her from such unwarranted *bile*!"

Before Liam could blink, Brigid lashed out and slapped him across the face with all of the strength she could muster. His cheek burned hot with pain where she had connected, but he did not move, for her words had rooted him to the spot.

"I dinna know what my father is up to, but I do know that Aileen and I are just as much at his mercy as Catriona is. She had nothing to do with anything, *anything* that my da may be a part of. But I will promise ye this. If my sister dies out there because yer cruelty drove her to run from ye, I will lay the blame of her death squarely at yer feet Liam MacDonell, and there will be a reckoning."

Brigid stormed out of the library and slammed the door shut behind her, leaving Liam alone with his regret and shame.

The hour was late as Liam sat by the roaring fire in Laird Drummond's library. He held a thick wool blanket wrapped snugly around his shoulders and stretched his long legs out towards the flames. The muscles in his calves and thighs ached from the hours of riding he had done that night in search of Catriona alongside of Laird Drummond's men. He flexed and curled the toes of his bare feet, placing them as close to the flames as he could without burning the skin of his soles. His sopping-wet socks lay flat next to his feet directly in front of the fire, and alongside them were a second pair of wet socks belonging to none other than Laird Drummond himself.

Liam looked down at the glass he held and gazed into the clear rich amber liquid. He took a sip of the whiskey, trying to savor how smooth it was, a delicate blend of smoke and honey. A bottle of it had been brought up from his host's personal collection, but he could not enjoy the complexity of flavors nor the warmth it made in the pit of his stomach after he had spent the last three hours outside searching for Catriona.

Liam looked over at Laird Drummond and took note of the drawn, tired expression on his face. The man stared deep into the fire and the light from the flames illuminated the worry lines that were etched deep into his forehead. The man looked as though he had aged a decade in that evening. His square powerful shoulders were hunched over in defeat and his burdens clouded his eyes.

Liam looked away, afraid that he would drown in the guilt that he had been mired in ever since Brigid had spoked to him. He could not deny that she had been right. Liam had driven Catriona to this, and now, because of his suspicion and short temper with her, his wife could very well pay for her freedom from him with her life.

"I'm sorry we did not find yer daughter, Drummond," Liam said quietly. Even as he spoke the words they sounded unworthy in his ears.

Laird Drummond took another large swallow of whiskey then stared down into the glass, swirling the liquid and studying it with such intensity, it was as though he were trying to divine his daughter's whereabouts from the depths.

"When she was born, she was just a wee bit of a thing, so much smaller than her two sisters had been. I was worried that she would not make it, ye ken. That God would see fit to take her from me. But then, my sweet lass looked up at me with her big blue eyes, and she grabbed my finger so tightly. It was then I knew she was made of sterner stuff. She's a kind heart, my wee Cat. And she is as gentle as the day is long, but she is not weak."

Laird Drummond finished off the whiskey in his glass and then reached for the bottle with unsteady hands. The deep amber liquid sloshed over the edge from the tremors, but Catriona's father paid them no mind.

"Three daughters," the man whispered before downing half the glass. Laird Drummond hacked and coughed from swallowing too much of the potent liquid too quickly, but the moment his throat was clear he took another large swallow. "I have three daughters," he repeated. "Do ye ken what it's like to have three daughters MacDonell?"

"I do not, no," Liam replied slowly. He kept a wary eye on his host as he watched the man refill his glass once more.

"Ye must protect them, MacDonell. Ye must be prepared to do anything for them even as ye worry they will turn around and hate ye for it. Ye do it because ye believe it to be for their own good. Three daughters, MacDonell. But by the saints, I never meant for it to go this far."

Drummond looked up from the glass and turned to him, his eyes wild and filled with sadness and regret. "They need husbands, MacDonell, and ye seemed a fine match for either of them. All I needed was for ye to take to one, just one." Without warning, his arm lashed out and he threw his glass into the fire.

The alcohol hit the flames and ignited, causing Liam to jerk back out of harm's way as tall flames burst out of the hearth.

"I did it," Laird Drummond said. "I forced Catriona into marrying ye. Oh God, I've been such a fool."

"Drummond," said Liam slowly, his stomach filling with dread. "What exactly did ye do?"

"I made a deal with the devil, lad." Laird Drummond shook his head. "I made a deal with the devil."

But before Liam could ask him what he meant by that, Laird Drummond slumped back into his chair with his eyes shut and began to snore.

CHAPTER 18

CATRIONA SAT STARING out the window of her chamber in Macnaghten's castle. She had slept deeply the night before due to pure exhaustion, but the fear of what was to happen to her had led to her night being full of uneasy dreams. No one had come to see or speak to her since she had been whisked away and her stomach was beginning to ache with hunger. The sun had long been up and though she was grateful for the solitude of not having her every movement watched as they had been on the journey here, she was beginning to wonder if they had simply forgotten about her.

She had laid her gown out to dry throughout the night but it was still damp the next morning. Putting it on had been incredibly uncomfortable, and as Catriona sat in the cold damp fabric, she cursed herself for ever leaving Invergarry. Maybe if she had just waited a little longer, she would have been able to find a way to talk some sense into Liam. Not that any of that mattered now. She had been wrong all along. For all of her championing of her father's innocence, there was no denying that he most likely did have something to do with Liam's troubles. If her father was willing to force Liam to marry her based on a lie, then it stood to reason he was capable of sending the reavers to plague his land. Even if this Macnaghten decided to release her, Catriona was not sure if she could go back to Drummond Castle now. If her father's actions had put her in this danger, how would she ever be able to look him in the eye again, let alone forgive him for what he had done both to her and to Liam. People had lost their lives and their homes. What could possibly be worth all of the pain he may have caused? She had to know the truth. What was going on here?

The sound of a key in the lock of her chamber door startled her from her thoughts and Catriona turned in her chair to see the portly figure of Laird Macnaghten fill the doorway.

"Lady Drummond, good morning," he said with a low bow.

All traces of the rage she had seen in him the night before had been erased, and in its place were the refined manners that Catriona had been raised to expect from a man of his station. Catriona eyed the man with uncertainty. She did not trust him nor his pleasant mood, but felt it would be wiser for her if she played along.

"Good morning, Laird Macnaghten," she stood to greet him with the air of a welcome guest. "Please forgive my appearance. I have had a very long and harried journey, and I arrived without a proper change of clothes."

Macnaghten looked aghast, but Catriona did not miss the look of glee that flashed in his eye. "I am so sorry, my dear. There was supposed to be a gown brought for ye early this morning. Are ye telling me that it never arrived? It was to be here with yer breakfast."

"I regret to inform ye that there was no gown, nor breakfast brought to me this morning."

Macnaghten walked toward her, his eyes trailing over the dirt and water stains of her ruined gown. He reached out and pressed the palm of his hand lightly to her forearm before brushing the dirt off on his plaid. "Unforgivable. Completely unforgivable. And to think," he said with a disapproving shake of his head, "ye've been forced to sit here in this damp rag all morning. Ye must be starving as well. No doubt yer used to much finer things. I ken that Laird Drummond spares no expense on his daughters. I'm sure that all three of ye are used to being spoiled by the man. I had a daughter once too, ye ken. Aye, she was the prettiest lass in all the highlands, and I loved her more than my own life. She was precious to me. But she's gone now." Macnaghten shook himself and smiled an empty smile at Catriona. His small round eyes were void of any joy, and all she felt as she stared back into them was a cold emptiness that sent a familiar unsettling feeling racing down her spine. "I will be sure food and a fresh gown is brought to ye right away."

With that, Laird Macnaghten turned and left the room.

Catriona waited patiently for the food and gown to arrive but they did not. Minutes slipped into hours and soon half the day had gone by without another person coming by. Macnaghten did not seem like the kind of man that would be very forgiving of his servants that did not follow his orders to the letter, which made Catriona wonder if he had told them to see to her at all. Late afternoon slipped into early evening and Catriona heard the key in the lock once more.

But this time it was not Macnaghten come to visit her but the same young girl that had opened the doors of the keep to them the night before.

"Pardon the interruption Lady Catriona, but I was told to bring ye yer dinner."

"Thank ye," Catriona told her politely. "What's yer name?"

"Anne," She said quietly.

"Thank ye very much, Anne,"

The girl looked up at her with fear in her eyes and whispered. "I dinna know if ye should be thanking me. What I bring ye is not fit for man nor beast. I dinna know what ye've done to make Laird Macnaghten so angry at ye, be unless yer starving I would not touch this unless I had no choice."

The girl removed the cloth from the plate of food and Catriona glanced down at it. The small slice of cheese was almost completely covered in mold, and the vegetables were rotten with black pits on them. Th slab of meat was grey and spotted, and the whole thing gave off a foul odor when she bent near.

"Oh!" Catriona covered her nose with her sleeve and turned away.

"Please take it away," she told the girl.

The young maid nodded and covered the plate once more.

"Why is he doing this to me?" Catriona asked as the maid left for the door.

"I dinna know, but he has been in a rage ever since ye showed up last night. He is not the kind of man ye want to have angry at ye." The girl hesitated a moment and then reached into her pocket. In a flash she threw something to Catriona, and Catriona snatched it out of the air. It was a soft fresh chunk of bread.

"I saved it from my own supper. Hurry and eat it before ye're caught otherwise I'll get the lash."

"Anne," she said softly, awed that the young girl would risk such a punishment for her.

"Whatever ye do, dinna anger him," the girl reminded her, before hurrying out the door and locking it behind her.

Catriona ate the bread quickly and stripped out of her gown and down to her shift. She no longer had any illusions that a clean gown would be coming for her that evening. The gown was mostly dry now at any rate. Catriona crawled into bed and curled up in a tight ball and willed herself to sleep.

CHAPTER 19

It was late morning the day after the search by the time the last of the rain finally stopped. When Catriona still had not arrived at the castle that morning, Laird Drummond called his men together to form a second search party.

The men split up into small groups in order to cover more ground. Traveling to the nearby crofts, they knocked on every door they came across, asking if anyone had seen Laird Drummond's daughter or sheltered her from the storm, but it was to no avail. Not a single person had seen her.

Dread crept into Liam's heart, and he begun to fear the worst. With there being no sign of Catriona in any of the homes near the castle, the men widened their search. Liam rode for half the day on the road back toward Invergarry, looking for any sign of her, but she was nowhere to be found.

The sun was setting by the time he made it back to Drummond Castle. His body was weary from the long day's ride, but more than that, his heart was heavy with worry. Guilt and burning shame gnawed relentlessly on his insides, and he did not know how he would be able to look Catriona's father and sisters in the eye.

Laird Drummond may have forced his hand when it came to marrying his daughter, but Catriona had been as innocent as he in the situation. She had tried to tell him so, but he had not wanted to believe it. And even after they had begun to grow closer, he had doubted her and betrayed her confidence and the first opportunity he had to prove himself worthy of her love.

And now she could be dead or injured somewhere, unable to call out for help. He wanted to hit something. Beat his hands against the stone walls of the keep until they bled, but it would do nothing to help Catriona, and very little to ease the turmoil inside of him.

Liam could hear the low murmuring sounds of conversation coming from the great hall. It was nothing like the booming joyous laughter and cheer that had filled the room the first time he had dined there two weeks ago. By now every castle inhabitant knew that Catriona was missing. It was no surprise that the news wore heavily on all of their hearts.

Liam stood in the doorway and looked at the sea of sullen distraught faces seated at the long rows of tables. There was not a single smile among them. He glanced up at the head table to see Laird Drummond looking sullenly down into his cup, the food in front of him completely ignored. Aileen was attempting to speak with her sister but Brigid was not looking at her, instead, she was looking at Liam, and the accusation in her eyes burned into him, filling him with a shame so acute that he had to look away.

Thinking better of entering the room, Liam had turned to leave when he heard heavy footsteps as someone ran down the hall.

"Laird MacDonell!" called the young stable boy who had

taken the care of his horse when he arrived back at the castle. "Lady Catriona," the boy panted, "her mare has just come back to the stable."

"She's here?" Liam asked, grabbing the boy by the shoulders. "Is she all right?"

The young boy shook his head. "She is not here sir, only her horse. I must tell Laird Drummond right away."

"Come on, then," said Liam, pushing the boy gently ahead of him into the hall.

The boy ran down the length of the tables as fast as his slender legs would carry him and dropped a quick low bow at the foot of the head table.

"Laird Drummond," the boy said, struggling to catch his breath. "Lady Catriona's horse just came back to the stable, but she was not on it. The horse does not appear to be injured, but it was loaded down with a pack of supplies. In it was a bit of food and what looked to be a man's shirt. I came to tell ye as soon as I saw."

"A man's shirt? Are ye certain lad?" Laird Drummond asked.

"Aye," the boy nodded frantically.

Laird Drummond stood up from the table.

"Da?" asked Brigid.

"Stay here with yer sister," he told her. "MacDonell, come with me. We need to talk."

Liam followed him out of the keep and into the manor house where Laird Drummond led him, past the large library where they had spoken the other night and into a smaller room.

In this room sat a large chair behind a wooden desk, though this one was much less ornate than the oversized desk which graced the library. Almost every inch of the surface was covered with scattered papers. Some appeared to be accounts and ledgers while others looked to be letters.

Laird Drummond scattered the papers with an impatient sweep of his arm, sending the majority of them cascading to the floor in his attempt to clear a spot on the desk.

"What is this all about, Drummond?" Liam asked impatiently.

Laird Drummond looked up at him with fear and anger in his eyes.

"I fear that Catriona has been taken," he said. "I did not want to suggest such a thing in front of her sisters. But it is the only thing that would explain her not arriving back here."

Liam nodded, thinking. "When she left I doubt very much that she would have taken the time to take one of my shirts with her, and where would she have gotten the pack? I think ye may be right. I hate to even think it, but someone may have taken her."

"Do ye think they will try to ransom her back to us?" Liam asked him.

"Aye, if they're smart. I fear there might not be more for us to do at this moment but wait to hear word of her." Laird Drummond rubbed both of his hands over his ruddy cheeks. "This is all my fault,"

"Nay, Drummond, no matter what I accused ye of, I see now that this is just as much my fault, if not more. I was the one that pushed her to this. I was the one that could not see a way to show the lass even a wee bit of kindness for days. And even when we did try to make peace I did not trust her fully. Maybe if I had, she would be safe at Invergarry right now."

Laird Drummond let out a heavy sigh and collapsed into his chair.

"Ye were right MacDonell," he said. He looked up and locked eyes with Liam, never wavering in his gaze. "What ye accused me of before. Aye, ye were right all along. I sent the reavers to ye. But I never told them to harm anyone," he was quick to defend. "They were under direct orders that no one was to get hurt. They were supposed to only be enough of a bother to ye that ye would eventually come seek me out for help. And then when ye did I would convince ye to wed one of my daughters."

Hearing the truth now, Liam wanted to be angry, but he found that all of his anger toward the man had already been spent.

"Why would ye do such a thing just to get one of yer daughters wed? Ye must know that it sounds like madness."

"I waited a long time before I fathered any children, MacDonell, and now my girls are grown, long past the time they should have been wed. I could not bear to part with them, ye ken? After a life spend fighting, they were a blessing to me. But I came to see that by keeping them with me so long, I was not doing them any favors. I have no sons to take over as Chief after I am gone. My daughters must be wed, so that I know they will be safe and looked after if anything were to happen to me."

"But why in Heaven would ye go to such lengths and deception, man? There must be more than a few lairds ye could have gone to. Why me? And why plague me with troubles to do it?"

"Ah well, ye see," Laird Drummond scratched his chin thoughtfully beneath his large grey beard. "That was not exactly my idea."

"Well then, whose idea was it?" Liam asked, now more curious than upset.

"I was corresponding with a friend, lamenting to him about my troubles, and it was his idea that ye would be suitable for one of my daughters. Though I had not known ye since ye were a lad, I ken well enough that yer clan had prospered under yer leadership. I told him that I was going to write to ye with my proposal for the union, but he told me he knew the make of ye, and that ye would never wed one of my daughters without cause. He convinced me that he had a way to make ye come to me, and that by wedding my daughters I would be doing ye the favor instead of the other way round. I have to admit, the man made a fine argument. And he was right, ye reacted exactly the way he said ye would. I was sure it was a blessed day when ye and yer brother walked through my door."

Unease slithered through Liam's gut like a thick oil as he listed to Laird Drummond's story.

"Tell me. Who is this friend of yours that kens the working of my mind so well?" he asked.

"That would be Laird Alexander Macnaghten. He said the two of ye were acquainted years ago."

Liam barely heard the last of what Laird Drummond said. There was a deafening roar in his ears as rage overtook him. He grabbed the second chair in the room, lifted it over his head, and threw it against the wall. A loud crack echoed through the room and the broken chair fell to the floor in pieces.

"Hold, MacDonell!" Laird Drummond shouted as he jumped up from his seat. "Get a hold of yourself, man!"

"The man who attacked Catriona on the night we met, who was he?" Liam shouted.

Laird Drummond sputtered, "I dinna see what that has to do with—"

"Who was he!"

"One of the reavers. Laird Macnaghten sent me some of his men so that if they were seen they would not be easily tied back to me."

"Why did he attack her?" Liam asked him.

"It was all planned. He would never have truly hurt my Cat, he was just meant to frighten her so that she would run toward yer room. That's why I placed ye where I did. It was all planned. In case ye did not agree to wed one of 'em."

Liam grabbed hold of the edge of the desk, his ragged breathing the only sound in the room.

"And who's idea was this plan? The plan to put Catriona in harm's way?" he asked, though he already knew the answer.

"Macnaghten," Laird Drummond said, sinking into his chair. "It was Macnaghten."

The room tilted beneath Liam's feet, and he held his hand out to steady himself.

"Ye've been played for a fool, old man," he whispered. "There is no doubt now that Catriona has been taken, and I know exactly who has yer daughter."

"No," Laird Drummond's voice shook. "Macnaghten would never! That's madness. Why would he do such a thing? I've never done anything to the man."

"Aye, ye probably haven't. But yer not the one he's trying to hurt. I have to go now."

"I'm coming with ye."

"No, I must do this on my own. I'll bring yer daughter back safe Drummond, and I promise ye that when I do, I'll care for her the way I should have from the start. Catriona should not be the one paying for our mistakes."

Laird Drummond grabbed him by the arm to stop him.

"Why does Macnaghten hate ye so? What did ye do to the man?"

Liam looked him in the eye without wavering. "I do not know for certain. But I have a suspicion it's to do with my first wife, Alana."

"Why the blazes would Macnaghten care about her?"

"Because he is her true father."

CHAPTER 20

Catriona awoke to the sound of boots shuffling on the floor of her chamber. Her eyes opened just as a large hand clamped down over her mouth, effectively muffling her screams. She thrashed about on the bed wildly, trying to free herself from the intruder. Her arms flailed blindly in the darkness as she tried to shove him away. The smell of onions filled her nose, the scent wafting up off of her assailants fingers.

"Quiet!" A voice hissed out. "Ye must be quiet lass, I'm not here to hurt ye. We need to get ye out of the keep, but I need ye to be calm."

The words slowly began to penetrate Catriona's haze of fear, and she stopped kicking and shoving against the man.

"There's a good lass," he said. He waited a moment, making sure that she really was calm and then slowly removed his hand from her mouth. "Ye must get dressed quickly."

"Who are ye?" Catriona asked as she climbed out of bed.

The man turned around to offer her some privacy, so Catriona was unable to see his face in the dim light.

"I dinna want ye to be afraid," he said to her.

"If ye are here to help me, then why should I be afraid? Tell me who ye are."

The man stepped out of the shadows and into the light that spilled in from the window.

Catriona gasped and took a step back when she saw that he was man who attacked her in her father's keep.

"Stay away from me!" Catriona told him.

The man held up both of his hands slowly where she could see them. "I promise ye that I am not going to attack ye. In truth lass, I was never going to attack ye that night either. I was not even truly drunk!"

"I do not understand what you mean." Catriona looked at him, confused.

"We dinna have time for this. I have to get ye out of here," he said.

"If you think that I am going to go anywhere with ye in the middle of the night, then ye had best make time to explain it to me. What do ye mean ye were never going to truly hurt me? And ye reeked of booze that night. Do ye think me a fool that I cannot tell a drunk man when I see one?"

"We dinna have time for this!" he said, frustrated.

Catriona crossed her arms over her chest and did not move.

"Blast!" the man whispered sharply. "If it will get ye to hurry up and come with me, then I'll try to explain it to ye. Yer father and Macnaghten came up with a plan to force MacDonell to marry one of Drummond's daughters. If the plan dinna work as it was supposed to, then I was meant to force ye into a situation that would make it appear ye had been compromised by MacDonell, and that's what I did. I was never going to hurt ye. Yer father paid me to scare ye enough to send ye in MacDonell's direction."

Catriona's mind raced. "But how would ye know where I would be? My being late for supper was a complete mistake."

"When ye went out painting that morning yer father was sure that ye would not make it back in time for Laird MacDonell's arrival. Yer father has been watching the man for weeks. The moment MacDonell set out for Drummond Castle yer father knew about it. Yer father and Macnaghten have been in it together from the start."

"But why would my father do such a terrible thing? None of this makes any sense!"

"I dinna know why yer father did it lass, in truth I barely know the man. It was Macnaghten that hired me originally. We were meant to do a wee bit of reaving to vex The MacDonell and that was all, no one was meant to get hurt. When yer father came to me about scaring ye, I had my doubts, but the money he offered was too good to turn down, ye understand. My wife's not been well, and it will go a long way to making her comfortable. But then it all went wrong. Last week, suddenly everything changed. Gavin set fire to those crofts and killed that family. He said he was acting under new orders from Laird Macnaghten. I'm telling ye lass, I never signed on for that. We were moving out of the area to make trouble somewhere else when Gavin and McNair stumbled across ye in the woods. I prayed that ye would not recognize me, but I knew it would do no good."

"So why are ye helping me now?" she asked.

"I dinna know what is wrong with Macnaghten, but the man's gone mad. He sent your horse to Drummond Castle this morning. McNair was to release it near yer father's land to let him know that Macnaghten has ya. I think the man plans to ransom ye back to yer father. But I dinna trust that no harm will come to ye in the time yer trapped here. I heard him and Gavin arguing. Gavin is the man's son, ye see. A bastard, but Macnaghten keeps him close. It sounded like they were fighting over a woman, Macnaghten's daughter, I suspect. But we've no time to get into that now. So do ye trust me enough to come with me now, lass? Because the longer we tarry here, the more chance we have of getting caught."

"Aye," said Catriona, hurrying for the door. "I've heard more than enough."

He whisked her out of the room and down the stairs, then turned down a narrow hallway which ended at a rough wooden door. When he reached the door, he knocked twice and it was quickly opened.

"What took ye so long?" a young maid whispered. Her brow furrowed with worry as she hurried them through the door and down the other set of stairs.

"It was my fault, I'm sorry," explained Catriona, hoping that the young girl would not end up in trouble with Macnaghten because of her.

"Never mind that now, just follow me."

She hurried them through the castle kitchens and out through to a back door. "This is where the food supplies come through. watch yer step, there is a bit of a dip just the other side of the door. Dinna trip."

They pressed themselves up against the castle wall and felt their way along. They had no lantern with them, not wanting anyone to see the light and become curious.

"All right this is as far as I can go,' the young girl told them. The horse is just across the way their behind there, tied to a post just around that corner. If ye hurry ye should make it out without anyone seeing ye. And don't forget this." The girl shoved a small bundle into Catriona's hands. "Some food for the journey. God go with ye, Lady Catriona."

And before Catriona could thank her, the girl turned and ran back to the kitchens.

They hurried across the small stretch of yard until they

found the horse exactly where the maid said it would be. Catriona wasted no time in climbing up and her rescuer climbed up behind her.

"I dinna even know yer name," she said to him as he guided the horse around and they took off into the night.

"Malcolm, m'lady," he said as the horse thundered away from Dunderaven Castle. "Ye may call me Malcolm."

Liam continued to ride through the night long after the sun went down. The roads were still muddy from all the rain, but he trudged on, determined to make it to Dunderaven by morning. It was the middle of the night, and he was weary from his long ride, but he was certain that he had finally crossed over onto Macnaghten lands. He shouldn't have much farther to go, and soon he would have Catriona safe again.

A rumbling sound reached his ears, and he listened closely to the sound of what could only be galloping hooves coming toward him. A few minutes later Liam saw a horse and rider come charging straight at him and he pulled off to the side of the road to avoid being run down. As they came closer, Liam saw a flash of bright hair whipping out behind the rider. A man sat atop the saddle behind her as they tore past him, but Liam had not mistaken that angelic face.

"Catriona!" he hollered, guiding his horse off the side of the road and went racing after Catriona and the man with her.

He pushed his horse faster and called her name again, "Catriona!"

Her horse slowed and the rider turned 'round to face him. After turning the horse, the man holding Catriona pulled out his sword and pointed it directly at Liam. "I dinna know who ye are," he hollered, "But ye'll not take her."

Liam brandished his sword and rode toward them. With one hand pointing the sword at Catriona's captor, he got close enough for them to see his face clearly.

He watched as Catriona's eyes widened at the sight of him, and her hands flew to her mouth as she gasped.

"I'll thank ye to unhand my wife," he said gravely.

"Laird MacDonell?" the man said in confusion.

"Aye, and ye have three seconds to tell me who ye are and where ye think ye're taking my wife before I remove yer head from yer shoulders."

"Liam?" Catriona said, her voice filled with confusion. "What are ye doing here?" she asked.

Liam was struck by the uncertainty in her eyes as she watched him warily.

"I feared Macnaghten had ye. I was coming to free ye. But it seems ye have gotten away without my help."

"Ye came for me? But why?"

The question came as blow to Liam. He had not known how it would feel to face Catriona again after how he had treated her. He had been so focused on getting her back unharmed that he had not thought about the fact that she may not want to see him again.

"I owe ye more apologies than I can count Catriona, and I swear ye'll be getting them but for now I think it's best that we make our way back to yer father's keep as soon as possible. I dinna want to be on the road when Macnaghten discovers that ye're gone."

"I dinna know if I want to go back there," she told him. "There have been so many lies..." she turned to look at the man behind her on the horse and then turned back to face Liam, "so much deception."

"Aye, I know. I've only just begun to learn the breadth of it myself. But Drummond Castle is closer than Invergarry, and I promised yer father that I would see ye home to him. He would never forgive me if I did not see ye back."

Catriona eyed him suspiciously. "Ye've spoken with my father?"

"Aye."

"And ye no longer want to go to war with him?" her suspicion was written clear across her face, and he could not blame her disbelief. But now was not the time to get into the details of the past few days.

"I was hasty in my actions, I'll not deny it, though my assumptions about him were not wrong. But yer father and I have come to a peace between us. All that matters to the both of us right now is that we get ye to safety." Liam held out his hand to her. "Come back with me. I'll see ye home."

Catriona looked at his outstretched hand and shook her head. "I'll come back to Drummond Castle with ye and see my father. But I'll not ride with ye. I'd rather ride with Malcolm. That is, if he does not mind."

"It would be an honor, m'lady," said Malcolm. "We should be going, it will be dawn in a few hours."

Liam eyed Malcolm suspiciously. "And just who are ye, Malcolm?" he asked.

"I..." Malcolm hesitated.

"He's the reason we were forced to wed," Catriona said. "Malcolm is the one who attacked me in the hall on the night we met."

Liam's eyes flew to Malcolm, but the man just shrugged before kicking his horse into a canter and riding off into the night, leaving Liam to follow behind, a dozen new questions racing through his head.

CHAPTER 21

By the time Drummond Castle was in sight, Catriona never wanted to find herself seated on the back of a horse ever again. She felt as though she had spent every day of the past two weeks wet, sore, or locked up against her wishes. But instead of relief at being back at her childhood home, she felt apprehension. While she looked forward to spending time with her sisters, she did not know what she would say to her father, or if she would even be able to face him.

People called her name and waved as she entered the courtyard, and she looked around, surprised by the exuberance of the welcome.

"They knew something had happened to ye," Liam told her. "They were worried, and are happy to see ye back safe."

Catriona nodded. Her smile was tight, but she waved to everyone as she rode by.

Someone must have run ahead to tell her father that they had returned, because as she climbed down from the horse, he burst into the yard with her two sisters following close behind him.

"Cat! My wee Cat, ye've come home to me!" Her father

swept her up into his arms and hugged her tightly. "Saints be praised, how I feared for ye, my girl. Are ye injured? Did that bastard Macnaghten hurt ye in any way?"

"No, Da, I'm not harmed—" she began, but was quickly cut off when her father squeezed her even tighter, making it difficult for her to breathe.

"My God, Cat. Can ye ever forgive me? I've been a right fool."

He set her back down on the ground and released her, but before she could answer him she was quickly enveloped by the arms of her sisters.

"How did ye get her back so quickly?" her father asked Liam.

"It was not me," Liam said. "In truth, she was already on her way back to ye when I came upon her."

"Ye escaped on yer own lass? But how?" Laird Drummond eyed his youngest daughter with a mix of curiosity and pride in his eyes.

Catriona looked around for Malcolm who was trying to edge away from the gathering crowd. He was most likely trying to avoid her father, but she was not going to allow his bravery go unrecognized. Not after what he had done for her.

"It was Malcom that freed me, Da, and saw me here safely. Though Liam escorted us on our way."

Her father's face paled at the sight of Malcolm, and he looked at his daughter with shame in his eyes.

"Catriona, I dinna know if he told ye..."

"Aye, Da, he did, but we can discuss that later, no? For now, I just want a bath, a change of clothes and to sleep for a week."

"I will go see to getting the water boiled for ye," said Aileen, hugging her tightly again and giving her a kiss on the cheek.

"And will ye see that Malcolm gets a warmth bath as well?" She asked her sister. "He deserves that and more, after all he's done for me."

"Aye," said Aileen, taking Malcolm by the arm. "I'll see to all of it."

Liam stood outside Catriona's chamber door and raised his hand to knock, but he could not do it. His hand hung there suspended in the air for a moment before he sighed in frustration, dropped his hand, and walked away. He had only gone a few steps before he stopped and cursed himself. Squaring his shoulders he marched back to her chamber door and knocked on it before he could change his mind again.

"Yes?" her voice called softly from the other side of the door.

"It's Liam. May I come in?"

There was a long pause before she finally replied, "Come in."

Liam entered the room to find Catriona sitting in her shift while Brigid stood behind her running a comb through Catriona's damp hair. She was a vision in flowing white. The fabric of her thin shift flowed over the gentle slopes of her body, hinting at the curves beneath.

He wanted to take her into his arms and hold her close. But although she sat there before him, she still felt as out of reach now as she had when she was missing.

"I was hoping to talk to ye for a moment," he told her.

Brigid set the comb down on the dressing table and placed her hand on Catriona's shoulder, giving it a gentle squeeze. "I'll leave the two of ye alone, then."

Brigid walked to the door and paused before Liam,

placing a hand lightly on his arm. "Thank ye," she whispered. "Thank ye for bringing her home to us."

Liam nodded silently, and Brigid took one final glance back at her sister before taking her leave. He felt like a fraud accepting her thanks. He hadn't brought Catriona back at all. His wife had found her own way back to them. He had never felt so useless as he had riding back to Drummond Castle alongside Catriona and Malcolm.

It was his job to protect her. A job that he had completely failed at performing time and time again. And now that he knew the full truth of their situation and her innocence in it, he feared that he would never be able to prove himself as worthy of the love and trust she had tried to offer him so many times, only to be rebuffed when his distrust got the better of him.

The door closed behind her, and suddenly he and Catriona we finally alone. "I hope that I'm not interrupting."

Catriona stood up and wrapped her arms tightly around herself.

"What did you want to discuss with me?"

Liam's heart clenched at the distrustful look in her eye. No matter what had happened to her over the last few days, he knew that he was the one to put that fear there. She had even preferred to be nearer to the man who had attacked her and put her in the position where she was forced to be wed in the first place. The truth of that stung, but if Malcolm had found a way to earn Catriona's trust, maybe there was hope for himself to do the same.

"I owe ye an apology," he told her. "In fact, I owe ye too many to count. I have been rude and unfair to ye since the day we wed, and there was no cause for it. Ye were not to blame. It was my pride, distrust and arrogance that put ye in such a dangerous position. Ye never should have felt the need to flee Invergarry. I'm hoping that, in time, ye can forgive me for all that I've done to ye, and that ye'll give me a chance to show ye that I can be the kind of husband ye deserve."

Catriona looked at him thoughtfully. "Do you mean that?" She asked quietly.

"Aye, I do. I'll be honest with ye. I have not fully seen ye for the person ye are. I've been too busy looking at ye through the pain of the past, but I see now that that's not fair to ye. Ye should not be made to pay for another woman's treachery and lies."

Catriona sat down slowly in the chair and clasped her hands in her lap. "Are you referring to your first wife?" she asked.

Liam's jaw clenched and his fists bunched at his sides. He did not want to speak of Alana, but after all that had passed between them, if there was one thing Liam owed Catriona, it was the truth. No matter how painful it may be. "What do ye know of my first wife?" he asked.

Catriona shook her head. "Nothing, really. Iain mentioned that you were wed once before when we traveled to Invergarry, but he would not tell me anything about her. He said it was not his place to share your secrets. The only reason he mentioned her, I believe, was simply because he wanted me to know that there was more behind your treatment of me than cruelty. That there was a pain you were still nursing. I think that he hoped it would make me a bit more understanding toward you and your actions."

"It's true that I was married before. I was young and foolish—and in love. The lass was a few years older than me, and enchanting in her beauty and her ways. I was bewitched by her from the first moment we met. It was not long before I asked her to marry me. My parents were both dead, and I had only recently taken over as Chief of clan MacDonell.

"It was not long after the wedding when she changed. She grew erratic. She would fly off into a temper without any warning and little provocation. She would disappear for days at a time. And then I began to hear the rumors. She was sneaking off to visit her lover. She had only married me for my power, and because I was young and so in love with her that she was sure she would be able to manipulate and control me. When I confronted her one evening about her dalliance, we argued, bitterly.

"And then, that night, when she was sneaking out again—I'm sure to see him—there was an accident. Her horse threw its shoe, and she was tossed from the saddle. She broke her neck upon impact with the ground. I was heartbroken and furious at the same time. When I contacted her father to inform him about what had happened, the man blamed me for his daughter's death. By that time, I knew that she had never loved me. I was simply a convenient means to an end."

"What was her name?"

Guilt flooded Liam but he took a deep breath and answered truthfully. "Alana. Alana Macnaghten."

"No!" Catriona gasped.

"Aye. And Catriona, there's more. I learned from yer father that it was Macnaghten who suggested to him that he should convince me to wed one of his daughters."

"I know. Malcolm told me."

"Malcolm. The man that attacked ye?" Liam asked skeptically.

"Aye. I know it does not make much sense. I've come to see that Malcolm is not a bad man, he just found himself in a bad situation that grew out of his control. In the end he risked his life to free me and bring me home, and I will be forever grateful to him for that. As I am grateful to ye as well. I know that ye set out after me to stop me from reaching my father to warn him of yer intentions. I know that ye do not care for me, and yet, ye came for me anyway, to free me from Macnaghten, even though leaving me to whatever fate he had planned for me could have ridded ye once and for all of a wife ye did not want."

Liam went up and knelt at Catriona's feet, taking her hands in his. "I may not have wanted to be wed, but I'm glad that yer my wife. And I may not have wanted to admit it to myself for fear of being played the fool again. but I do care for ye. I've had a glimpse of who ye are, who ye truly are through yer sister's and yer father's eyes. And I see the love held for ye by the people who live in the castle. But I no longer want to see ye through their eyes. I want to take ye home, back home to Invergarry with me. And I want to get to know ye for myself. And I would like very much for ye to get to know me. If ye'll give me the chance."

Liam's heart pounded in his chest, afraid that she would not be able to find it in her heart to forgive him. The seconds slipped by, stretching out into eternity.

Catriona bit her bottom lip, taking a moment to consider before finally answering. "Aye, I would like that very much."

CHAPTER 22

THE NEXT MORNING, Catriona walked into her father's library where she found Liam sitting at the desk opposite her father, the two of them deep in conversation.

"But what are we going to do about him?" her father asked.

"We cannot let this stand," said Liam. "For all I know, he will continue paying those men to torch my land. If ye say ye did not want anyone to get hurt, then it is obvious Macnaghten has plans that do not involve you."

"Da?" Catriona asked.

Both men looked up at her in surprise, as neither had heard her enter the room.

"Catriona, I thought ye might be sleeping for a while yet," her father said. "Ye must recover. These last few weeks must have been trying on ye."

She brushed a loose strand of hair back from her face and tucked it behind her ear, suddenly feeling self-conscious about the dark circles she had beneath her eyes and the pallor of her skin. "I was feeling restless. I've spent more time than necessary in bedchambers as of late," she told him.

Catriona's eyes flicked over to Liam for a moment before darting away again.

Liam stiffened in his seat, and even through her ire, Catriona's heart went out to him. She had not meant to guilt him, but having your husband lock you in your bedchamber was not something one soon forgot.

Hurt at his actions and her forgiving nature battled within her. He had come for her. And while she may have found another means of escape, the thought of him confronting Macnaghten on her behalf and demanding that the treacherous Laird release her at once sent a shiver of a thrill through her body.

Hesitantly she moved towards Liam, rested her hand on his shoulder for a moment, and squeezed it gently in reassurance before quickly removing it.

"What have the two of ye been discussing?" she asked.

"Nothing that ye need to worry about, lass," said her father. "Have ye seen yer sisters this morning? I know they would love to spend some time with ye."

Catriona's face flushed red as anger began to bubble up inside of her. Once again the men were dismissing her as if she had nothing of value to contribute. As if the only thing she was good for was being bartered, ransomed, or rescued. Refusing to be brushed aside so easily, she sat down in the chair beside Liam, across from her father.

"Is it Laird Macnaghten then?" she asked.

"Now, Catriona," said her father, "I do not want to upset ye, lass."

"Da," Catriona said quietly. "I understand ye want to protect me. But after what I've been through this past week, I cannot just... I cannot just ignore what happened."

"Neither can we, lass," said her da. "That's why Liam and I are discussing what to do about Macnaghten."

"Are ye sure that he will not just leave us alone now?" she asked.

"I dinna think that is very likely," said Liam. "It sounds like he has been planning this for some time. I did not realize that he still held such hatred for me. But for him to come up with such an elaborate, plan... it is unlikely that he will give up so easily."

"But we know that he is the one behind the destruction on your land now. When I arrived at Dunderaven, he was furious that I had been brought to him. He didn't want it known that he was in acquaintance with the men who had kidnapped me. He said something about exposing him, and his entire plan being at risk."

"It looks like he is not finished with ye, lad," said her father.

"Yes, but surely once he realized I had escaped Dunderaven, he must have suspected that I would have told you where I had been? Would he really risk continuing on, knowing that he is most likely exposed and no longer has my father to hide behind?"

"Laird Drummond, Macnaghten used yer desire to have yer girls wed to his advantage, but do ye have any idea why he would want to see me married?"

"Maybe he just wanted to see ye suffer?" said Catriona. "He has been suffering the loss of his daughter all of these years. Maybe now he wants you to know what it would feel like to be trapped in a marriage of hate."

"Well, whatever it is, I cannot stay here much longer," said Liam. "I must return home to find out how my brother's injuries fare. I am praying that he has recovered some by now." He looked at Catriona. "I have no doubt that ye would like to spend more time with yer family, but we must return as soon as possible."

Catriona nodded. "I understand. Once we have seen to

yer brother, ye will be free to pursue Macnaghten with a clear mind."

Catriona stood to take her leave when a memory struck her. "Did either of ye know that Macnaghten has a son?"

"Are ye sure, lass?" asked Laird Drummond. "I had not heard of him fathering any children."

"It's true. The leader of the group, the one that burned down the home and injured Alex. I found out that he is in fact Macnaghten's son. He is illegitimate and Macnaghten has not seen fit to grant the man his name. His name is Gavin. He was a terrifying man. I hope to never lay eyes on him again."

"Ye never will," Liam said firmly. "I can promise ye that."

"Liam," her father said, "I know ye're eager to see how your brother fares, but Macnaghten must be dealt with now, before things grow even more out of hand. Catriona will be safe here, ye know that as well as I. Let her spend some time with her sisters while we ride to Dunderaven and deal with this, once and for all. Macnaghten must be held accountable for all that he has done, and I would not want to give that man any more time to put his schemes in motion."

Liam sat silently for a moment before nodding in agreement. "Ye're right, this cannot wait any longer. Let us find out what Macnaghten is truly after, once and for all."

Liam had never before been to Laird Macnaghten's keep, having never had need to pay visit to the man or his modest lands, and as he and Laird Drummond dismounted their horses in the courtyard, he hoped to never have to come back to Dunderaven again. There was something about the place that he found unsettling. There was a heaviness in the air of the courtyard that made the hair on the back of his neck stand on end. It was as if the all joy and laughter had been beaten out of the place and all who dwelled there. As Liam glanced around, he saw that there was nary a smile or bright face to be found. The residents moved around the courtyard at a hurried pace, their eyes downcast as they went about their tasks.

What had Macnaghten done to his people to leach the life out of them in such a way?

"Mind yourself, lad," said Laird Drummond, as the two of them made their way into the keep.

"Can I help ye?" a man asked as they walked into the entry way, his eye on the colors of their plaids.

"Aye," said Liam. "We're here to have a word with Laird Macnaghten."

"I believe his lairdship is in his office. Is he expecting ye?"

"I believe, not, but the matter is urgent, and he'll be wanting to hear what we have to say."

The man stared at them silently for a moment before finally jerking his head in a sharp nod. "I'll show ye the way."

"Thank ye," said Laird Drummond.

Liam and Laird Drummond followed the clansman up a winding staircase until they reached the top floor of the keep. At the end of the hallway was a tall door inlaid with brass bars.

What manner of threat could Macnaghten fear to feel the need to reinforce the door to his study in such a way?

The clansman knocked heavily on the door and they waited for a moment with no response. Liam could hear rushed shuffling behind the door before a harried voice finally barked out, "Yes?"

"There are men here to see ye, Laird Macnaghten. They say it's urgent."

"Who is it?" Macnaghten shouted.

The clansman blanched, realizing that he had not gotten their names.

Liam was growing tired of the delay. He reached out and tested the handle of the door to the chamber. When he gave it a push, he was surprised to find the door unbarred. If the man was to have a reinforced door, how could it be possible that he did not even possess the sense to lock it? Of course, who among his men would be foolish enough to enter the room unbidden, especially when he resided on the other side? But Liam was not one of his men, and after all of the trouble Macnaghten had caused, he most certainly did dare to enter the man's study without being given leave to do so.

"Ye cannot—" the clansman tried to stop him, but Liam cut him off, shoving him aside and barging into Macnaghten's study with Laird Drummond directly on his heels.

Laird Macnaghten jumped to his feet behind his desk at the unwelcome intrusion. "Just what in God's name do ye think ye're doing, barging in here like this?"

"Sit yerself down, Macnaghten," Liam growled. "Laird Drummond and I would have a word with ye."

"Laird Macnaghten, sir—" the clansman began apologetically, but Macnaghten held up his hand to silence him.

"Get out," said Macnaghten.

"But, sir..."

"I said, get out." Macnaghten hissed. "Do not make me have to tell ye again."

"Aye, sir," said the clansman. With a final suspicious glance at the visitors, he hurried out of the room and shut the door behind him.

"So," said Macnaghten, "what brings the two of ye to Dunderaven? Laird MacDonell, I do believe I heard a rumor that congratulations are in order. Should ye not be at home with yer lovely bride?" Macnaghten's eyes beady eyes crinkled at the corners as the corner of his thin mouth turned up in a sneering smile, and his eyes twinkled with mischief.

"And just how would ye have come to hear about my marriage, then, Macnaghten?" Liam asked him, keeping his voice as level as possible, even as his fingers twitched to wrap themselves around the short, portly man's fat neck.

"Well, ye know how news travels in the highlands. And I pride myself on being well informed."

"Aye well, ye may not be so well informed as ye think."

"Oh aye, and why is that?"

"Enough of this," said Laird Drummond. His face was thunderous as he stared down the man across the table from him. A man he had once counted among his friends. "Ye sit there making quips, when not one week ago, ye held my youngest daughter hostage. I ought to run ye through where ye sit, ye coward."

"Ye dare call me a coward?" Macnaghten roared.

"Aye, I do! Using my sweet daughter for yer own twisted deeds. What are ye about man, pitting me and MacDonell against one another? What do ye have to gain by causing discord between us?"

"The only thing I've wanted these past ten years." He turned to Liam with fury and disgust in his eyes. "Your suffering."

"Have ye gone completely mad?" Liam demanded.

"Madness? Is it madness to want to see justice done? Is it madness for a father to want to avenge the life of his only daughter? I had one daughter. ONE. And she was more precious to me than life itself. But I could not be with her as a father should. I could not raise her and guide her, no, that gift was bestowed upon another. And what did that man do with my precious child? He allowed her to be married to you! Ye wed my sweet Alana and ye destroyed the light within her! Ye crushed everything in her that was good and kind until she could bear the heavy blows of yer fists no longer. Do not think to deny it! God knows the truth of her deeds! Yer violent ways drove my sweet lass to take her own life. She knew it was the only way for her to be free of ye forever. And when I discovered what you had driven her to, I vowed that I would make the rest of yer life a miserable one, and I would destroy everything that ye held dear."

"Ye spread nothing but lies," spat Liam. "Falsehoods drip from yer lips like venom from a snake's fangs. Not once did I ever raise a hand to Alana. Ye speak to me of a father's love? For most of her life she did not know ye were her true father. She did not know the truth of who ye were until she was long grown. And she ken that she had to keep the secret of her parentage, oh aye, she ken. But she admitted it to me one night in a fit of rage when she was well into her cups. Screamed at me how I would never be as great a leader as her true father Laird Macnaghten. And though I could hardly believe it, I recognized it for the truth it was. She had had so much to drink that evening I highly doubt she remembered revealing it to me the next morning, and we never mentioned it again. But I find it laughable that you expect me to believe you have ever harbored even a kernel of fatherly affection towards her after you lied to her for her entire life."

"The lass was mine, my own! And ye as good as killed her."

"No, I did not!" Enraged, Liam grabbed a ledger from atop the desk and hurled it at the wall. The force of the impact knocked pages from the book and they went scattering to the floor.

"Alana did not kill herself, she was thrown from her horse and broke her selfish, vicious neck. The lass was no sweet girl, as ye're wont to believe. She had a heart as cold as stone and a cruel calculating mind. She fooled me. Aye, I'll admit it, much to my shame. She fooled me into thinking that she was in love with me and so, foolishly, I fell in love with her. But she was only using me for my wealth and position. As soon as our vows were made, she revealed herself for the calculating harpy she truly was. Do ye want to know the truth of where she was riding to the night she died? To see her lover. Aye, she cuckolded me and made me a fool."

"Lies," hissed Macnaghten.

"The truth!" shouted Liam. "All yer pain and rage, yer need for vengeance that ye've focused on me. It is based on nothing. I loved Alana, though she did not deserve it. I even mourned her after she was gone. And I may not have been the man she truly wanted, but I will not have the blame of her death laid at my door."

"This... this cannot be." Laird Macnaghten shook his head slowly and sank back down into he's chair.

Liam almost pitied the sunken, defeated man. Almost.

"It is over, Macnaghten," said Laird Drummond.

"Aye," agreed Liam. "Let Alana's spirit rest at last. Put an end to your schemes and leave my people in peace. Her men took the homes and lives of some of my clansmen, and for that they must be brought to justice. I can see how Alana's death has been torturing ye for all these years, and maybe the pain ye feel is justice enough if ye promise that this will be the end of it. But if I go home to discover that my brother Alex is not on his way to recovery, it will be war between us. I promise ye that."

CHAPTER 23

"So, it is over then?" asked Catriona. She sat at her dressing table and carelessly ran a comb through her hair as she listened to Liam's story of confronting Laird Macnaghten with her father, more interested in their encounter with the scheming Laird than prepping her hair for sleep.

"Aye, it's over. At least for now. I still have to see how Alex fares when I get home. He's a strong man, my brother, but I fear that I've been away from him for too long."

"After everything that he has done, all the pain that he has caused, there is a small piece of me that must admit, I almost feel sorry for Laird Macnaghten. I cannot imagine the pain he must have felt to have lost his daughter like that. He could not claim her as his own. He could not confront you man to man. And to believe for all of these years that you were the cause of her death? It's no wonder that it drove him a little bit insane."

"I hear what you are saying, but I will not make excuses for the man. Beyond the thefts, his actions cost innocent people their lives. He will need to be held accountable for that."

"But we do not have any proof of his actions."

"I know. and it is highly unlikely that we will be able to force him to confess his deeds to anyone other than your father and me. But at least his men will see the inside of a jail cell for what they have done. There will be a little justice at least."

Catriona turned to look at him. The shadows beneath his eyes were deep and he looked weary, as though he had just come home from a battle long fought. And in a way, she supposed he had. The reavers had been plaguing his land for months now, and finally there was an end in sight. But what victory could there be if he lost his brother in the process? How would he ever be able to find any peace? Alana's selfishness and death had sent ripples through their lives like the waves in a pool after a stone had been dropped in it. The choices she had made had shaped not only her own fate, but the fate of so many people around her. And now, years later, Liam's brother could possibly pay the ultimate price for the decisions that she had made.

"Let's go home tomorrow," she said to Liam.

Liam look startled at her words. "Home?"

Catriona nodded and stood up, moving towards him. She took both his hands in hers and looked up into his weary eyes. "Aye, home, to Invargarry. You should not be away from your brother for much longer. You have already spent too much time away."

"Home?" he asked again, stretching the word out as though it were foreign on his tongue.

Catriona could not blame him. Invergarry had felt like more of a prison than a home the last time she was there, but this time it would be different. They would make it different.

"Yes," she told him. "Home. Your home is now mine. I'm

looking forward to putting all of this behind us and starting afresh. Of having a life with you. Being your wife. Bearing your children." She blushed a little at that but did not waver from his gaze. "You said that you had begun to see me for who I really am through my family's eyes. Well, I believe that I have begun to see who you truly are as well."

"Oh, and who is that?"

Her heart warmed at the hint of hope in his voice and she squeezed his hands. She ran her thumbs over the backs of them, strong and weather-worn. Against her palms she could feel his calluses. They were the result of years of hard work, wielding a blade and leading his people.

"You came for me. You did not fully trust me, ye did not really know me, and yet, when I needed ye, when I was taken, ye came for me. My sister's told me of how ye searched for me through the storm. Ye came to Dunderaven to find me. And I have no doubt that if I had not already been freed ye would have done everything in yer power to get me back." She stared into the depths of Liam's grey eyes and could feel tears forming in her own. "I do not know if ye even realized it, but when you saw me with Malcolm and drew your sword on him, you called me 'wife.' It was the first and only time that you called me your wife instead of by my name. And hearing that word on your lips made my heart swell. I had not realized before just how badly I had been wanting to hear it. That I had been longing to feel like a true wife to you. But I do. I want to be a wife to you. To stand by your side, to hold your trust and your love. For us to be a family. I want to love you, Liam MacDonell. Will you let me do that?"

Catriona gasped when Liam pulled his hands from hers, only to find herself enveloped in his strong arms, crushed against his chest. His hands were in her hair, tilting her head back as he lowered his own, pressing his lips against hers.

This kiss was nothing like the sweet kiss they had shared

on the banks of Loch Oich. His mouth was hungry and his tongue forceful, prying her lips apart and demanding entry to her inexperienced mouth. Catriona moaned and tentatively sought his tongue with her own, urging him on. Her head spun, and she felt the earth tilt beneath her feet and she held tightly to him to keep herself upright as he plundered her mouth. A curious urge overtook her and she pulled back slightly and nibbled on his lower lip ever so lightly.

Liam groaned and slid a hand down her back to cup her bottom, squeezing it and pressing her closer to him. She could feel the hardness of him through the front of her gown and her entire body flushed with heat. She had never desired a man before the way she did him. She wanted to feel him. To feel all of him. To know what it would be like to finally become a woman. *His* woman.

She ran her hands up his arms and down the broad expanse of his chest, feeling the hard muscles beneath her fingertips through the coarse material of his shirt. She could feel the warmth radiating off of him, and she longed to touch his bare skin. Feeling emboldened, she reached lower and took a large bunch of material in her hand and began pulling his shirt out from where it was tucked into his plaid. Once the front of his shirt was free, she hesitated for a moment, unsure of whether she should continue, whether she was taking things too far, but she wanted to know. She had to feel him. Holding her breath, she slipped her hands beneath his shirt and pressed them to the flat of his stomach. She felt his muscles contract at her touch, and he pulled his lips away from hers slightly.

"God, Catriona, ye drive me wild," he groaned.

"You do the same to me," she told him.

Liam lifted her off the floor with his arms wrapped around her hips and carried her to the bed where he stood her on top of it in front of him. Catriona stared at him, her eyes wide. as he ran his hands up the slope of her hips, along her waist, and up her sides until they rested alongside her breasts.

Her breathing became shallow and ragged. She could feel her nipples hardening in anticipation of his touch, but he did not move his hands to cup her breasts. She watched, wide-eyed, as instead, he leaned forward and placed his lips gentle against her collar bone. Catriona's eyes fluttered closed, and she focused on the sensation of his warm lips moving up her throat and over her skin until he reached her shoulder where he placed a gentle kiss.

Her heart pounded as his lips continued their path of discovery back to up to her jaw where he place gentle kisses from one side of her face, to her chin, to the other side of her jaw and back down her throat. Never in her life had Catriona been handled so sweetly, treated so gently. She could hardly believe that the tenderness she was experiencing was coming from Liam.

His hands moved to the laces of her gown, and he began undoing them, leisurely taking his time as he undressed her until finally, the gown gave way and she was standing in nothing but her shift, with her gown pooled on the bed around her ankles.

Liam stepped back and took in the sight of her, devoured her with his eyes. She had never seen such longing in them before.

"Ye are so beautiful. I've never seen eyes the color of yers before. On our wedding day, even as I cursed ye for having trapped me against my wishes, I looked into yer eyes and said to myself that I had never seen eyes so incredible before in all my life. I could drown in your eyes, Cat. I could lose myself in them, in you, never come up for air and die a happy man."

A tear rolled down Catriona's cheeks at his words, and he brushed it away, then kissed her on the lips again, more gently than he had before. She wrapped her arms around his neck and pulled him closer, never wanting to let him go.

His hands stroked her calf and slid up the back of her leg, lifting her shift as he went, exposing more and more of her skin to him. She gasped as the cool air hit her flesh, but it was soon warmed by the firm touch of his hands.

"I want ye, Cat," he groaned into her mouth. "God help me, I want ye so bad."

His hands became more insistent as he tugged at the fabric, lifting it up above her waist. She released him and raised her arms above her head, allowing him to undress her. Liam pulled the shift off of her in one smooth stroke and dropped it on the floor, forgotten at his feet.

Catriona suddenly felt vulnerable, standing before her husband in nothing but her skin and instinctively moved to cover her breasts with her arms.

"No," he said, stopping her with a hand on her arm. "Do not hide yourself from me. Ye are a vision." He drank in the sight of her, his eyes roaming g over every inch of her exposed flesh. Catriona's breathing increased as he reached out to her, and then ever so gently took one of her breasts in the palm of his hand. He stroked the underside of her breast with his palm and then ran his thumb over her hardened nipple. It was so sensitive that she had to close her eyes. She could feel him moving toward her, closing the distance between them when suddenly, she felt his mouth replace his thumb and close around the nipple. He took it into his mouth, his tongue flicking at it, as he held it between his teeth. Never before had she felt something so wonderful. How could love making get better than this?

Her question was soon answered as Liam lifted his hand and placed it on her thigh, holding it there unmoving for a moment, before inching his way closer to the centre of her and slipping his fingers between her legs.

"Oh!" she cried out, as he pressed his fingers against her heat.

He bit down gently on her nipple as he rubbed his fingers rhythmically against her most sensitive area causing a thunderous turmoil to build inside of her like she had never experienced before. Her legs began to shake, and she grabbed onto his shoulders for balance, fearful that she would fall, unable to hold herself up under her own strength for much longer.

Suddenly, his fingers and mouth were gone from her skin and Catriona whimpered in protest, but Liam merely scooped her up and lay her down on the bed before he began kissing the soft skin of her stomach. He covered every inch of it in kisses as his fingers began to slowly stroke in between her legs once more. He kissed lower on her stomach, and down over her mound until the heat of his eager mouth joined his clever fingers between her thighs.

"Spread yer legs wider for me, love," he encouraged, his voice was deep, rough and insisting, there was nothing she could do but obey him. Opening her legs wider, she gasped and arched her back as Liam pressed his tongue to her wet flesh, swirling it around the hard little nub and sent her senses spiraling out of control.

She cried out, clutching at the bed clothes, her head thrashing side to side as wave after wave of pleasure engulfed her. She was sure that she would buck him off, but Liam held tight to her waist and would not allow her to wriggle her way free from the overwhelming sensations he was causing within her.

All too soon, the thunderous wave of pleasure receded,

and she sank back down onto the bed panting for air. Liam moved up and laid down beside her, wrapping his arm tight around her and pulling her in close until she was nestled snugly against his body.

"But, you didn't..." Catriona trailed off, unsure of how to ask. "I thought that you would need to..."

Liam chuckled and pressed a kiss to the top of her head. "The first time I have ye fully as my wife, I want it to be beneath the roof of Invergarry. I want it to be in our home."

Catriona smiled into his chest and snuggled closer still. *Our home.* Two simple words had never sounded so sweet.

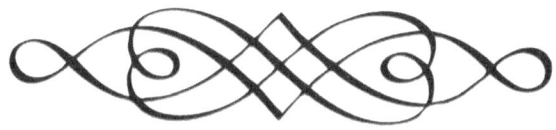

CHAPTER 24

CATRIONA SAT in her father's library idly eating a slice of bread with jam and reading a book when her sisters rushed in to greet her.

"You're leaving!" Brigid accused. "How can you possibly be leaving already? You've only just arrived!"

"I know," said Catriona, setting down her snack. "How did you find out already"

"We overheard Laird MacDonell speaking with Da about it at breakfast," said Aileen. "A meal for which you were noticeably absent."

Cartiona looked away and blushed, unable to meet her sister's questioning gaze. "Were you not feeling well this morning then? Or was it just that you do not want to spend more time with your new husband than you have to?"

Catriona's blush deepened and she shook her head. "No, it is not that," she said. "I was just sleeping so soundly that I did not wake in time to come downstairs, and Liam didn't bother to wake me."

"So he left you up there to starve did he?" asked Brigid with a snort.

"You know, he is not so bad as you think," said Catriona, picking an invisible piece of thread from the skirt of her gown. "He can be actually quite sweet when he wants to be."

Her sisters exchanged a skeptical look between them and crossed the room to sit with her.

"'Sweet' is not the term that comes to my mind when I think of Liam MacDonell," said Aileen.

"Nor I," Brigid agreed.

"I will not deny that we were thrown together under less than ideal circumstances. And if I had been given the opportunity to choose a husband of my own, he would not have been the one that I had picked for myself. But now that we have had some time to learn the truth of one another he is much more... pleasant."

"Pleasant?" said Aileen.

"And... gentle," Catriona added, her mind wandering back to the night before, and the memory of the way Liam's lips had grazed the tender skin of her throat.

"Gentle?" Brigid parroted.

Catriona pulled herself from her daydream and cleared her throat. "Yes, pleasant and gentle. And whether you believe me or not, I am telling you now that I am happy that he is my husband, and given the choice, I would not trade him for any other."

Brigid narrowed her eyes at Catriona, unsure if she fully believed what her sister was saying, then eventually gave a small shrug. "So long as you are no longer unhappy about what Da did then I suppose it has all worked out all right. But I'm telling you now, if our father ever tries something like that with me, I will make him sorry that he ever tried."

"Oh hush, Brigid," Aileen scolded. "If father sees fit to see you wed, we both know that you will do your daughterly duty and marry whomever he picks."

"I would rather kiss a frog." Brigid folded her arms across her chest and sat back in her chair.

"Well," said Aileen sweetly, "depending on the man you have to marry it may just feel like you are anyway."

Brigid reached for a small cushion and hit her sister with it.

"Ow!" shouted Aileen, feigning injury.

Catriona threw back her head and erupted with laughter. She had not felt so carefree in a long time. It felt like almost another lifetime now. She would miss her sisters when she left, but it warmed her heart to know that they would at least have one another to keep each other company. Brigid did have a point though. What if their father did try to force her sisters to marry? She shook her head, ridding herself of the idea. After all that had passed, and everything that had gone wrong, she could not believe her father to do anything so foolhardy again.

As though summoned by her very thoughts, Laird Drummond's large frame suddenly filled the doorway.

"What's going on in here, then?" he asked, looking around at the commotion in the room. "I could hear the three of you clear down the hallway."

He strode across the room and kissed each of his daughters on the top of their heads.

"Oh nothing, Da," Catriona said with a hiccupping laugh. "We've just been in here discussing Brigid's desire to kiss frogs."

Their father's head turned sharply, to Brigid, a look of alarm on his face, causing Catriona and Aileen to burst into renewed paroxysms of laughter.

"Oh, you're terrible, the both of you!" shouted Brigid, retaking up the cushion as a weapon and throwing it at Catriona.

"Hey now!" said Laird Drummond. "Brigid! Is that any way to act like a lady?"

"But! But... Da!" Brigid sputtered.

Catriona giggled and winked at Brigid, whose face was now almost as red as her hair.

"Oh!" Brigid fumed and jumped up from the chair. "You always were the favorite."

"Now, now," said their father, "Ye all know that I have no favorites among ye. I love ye all equally."

"Just as I love my sisters equally," said Catriona. She stood up and wrapped her arms around Brigid in a tight embrace. It had always been easy to get Brigid's anger up when they teased her, but thankfully for her and Aileen, she never stayed upset with them for long, knowing that it was all in good fun. Brigid returned Catriona's embrace with one of her own and held her sister tight.

"Are you sure that you must be leaving us so soon?" Brigid asked sadly.

"Aye. It's time for Liam and me to return to Invergarry. But I very much hope that you all will come to visit me soon. I will be missing you fiercely."

Aileen stood and wrapped her arms around both of her sisters, not wanting to be left out of the farewell. "We will come and visit you as soon as we can. I promise. Just promise me that you will be happy."

"I will," Catriona told her. "I am."

"You are?" Laird Drummond asked and the girls turned to face their father, releasing one another.

"Aye Da, I am. Do you mind if I have a moment alone with Da?" she asked her sisters. "There are some things that I feel need to be said before Liam and I are on our way."

Her sisters nodded before giving her another quick hug and heading for the door. "We'll see you off when it's time to go," said Aileen.

Catriona nodded and waited silently while her sisters left the room before turning to face her father.

"Cat..." her dad said.

Catriona took hold of one of her father's hands and smiled at him. "Da, I understand why you did what you did."

"You do?" he asked.

"Aye, Liam explained it all to me. And while I do not agree with it, I cannot hate you for it either. You have always been a wonderful father to my sisters and me. I know that you feel guilty for allowing Macnaghten to take advantage of you, but you could never have foreseen something like that. And I want you to know that I'm happy. I believe that Liam and I will have a good life together."

Laird Drummond smiled a wide smile, the twinkle returning to his eye. "So it all worked out for the best then."

"But before I go Da, I want you to promise me one thing. Promise me that you won't trick Brigid or Aileen into marriage like you did with me. Please don't make them have to go through what I did."

"Now, Cat, I promise ye that I will never do anything so foolhardy again. You have my word."

"Thank ye, da."

Laird Drummond opened his arms and hugged his youngest daughter.

"All worked out for the best," he mumbled.

"What was that, da?"

"Nothing, Cat, nothing at all."

Liam reached over to Catriona on the horse next to him and patted her on the thigh. "It won't be much longer now," he told her. The two of them had made good time on their way back to Invergarry. The weather had held, and they had enjoyed warm spring days the entire length of their journey.

"I am looking forward to seeing your brother again, and finding out how Alex fares." She went silent and her mouth turned down in a frown.

"What is it?"

"What is the name of the serving maid," she asked him softly.

"Which one?"

She looked at him, and tilted her head to the side. "You know which one, Liam. The poor girl that I tied up when I made my escape. I must find her and apologize to her straight away. The poor thing was scared out of her wits. I feel so terrible about what I did to her. I just didn't feel as though I had a choice."

Liam nodded. "Mary has already forgiven ye, Cat. She knows that ye meant her no harm, she told me so herself."

Catriona let out a sigh, and relaxed her shoulders, some of her tension leaving her. "I'm glad to hear it, but I would still like to make amends. I owe her that much."

"I understand your wanting to make things right with her. Ye've got a good heart, Cat. Her name is Mary."

Catriona opened her mouth but her answer was cut off in a strangled gasp.

There on the side of the road in front of them was a grisly sight. Four men were tied to thick posts staked into the ground. As the two of them rode closer, Liam could see that the men's throats had been cut. He could not tell how long they had been left like that but it was obvious that the birds had begun to circle the bodies, as the eyes were missing from two of the dead.

"Oh, Liam," Catriona gasped, her hand flying to her mouth, "how awful."

And it was at that. The closer he got he saw that having

their throats slit was not all that had been done to the men. But there, carved into each of their foreheads was the letter 'A'.

"What do you think it means?" Catriona asked him, unable to take her eyes off of the horrible scene.

"I dinna know."

"Liam..."

"One moment, I need to get a better look," he told her, nudging his horse closer to the bodies. "Who would do this? And to leave them displayed in such a way? It's barbaric."

"Liam," Catriona said again, this time more insistent.

"What is it?" Liam turned to her and stopped when he saw how pale her face was. Her eyes were fixed on the bodies as though she were seeing a ghost. "Catriona, Cat, what's wrong? Are ye going to be sick, lass?"

"Liam, I know these men! These are the men who took me."

"Are ye sure these are the same men?" Liam looked up at each of the corpses and studied their faces intently.

"Yes, I'm sure," Catriona whispered. "They were not faces that I am ever likely to forget."

Liam could not draw his gaze from the 'A' engraved on each man's forehead.

"This must be Macnaghten's work."

"Do you think that he killed them?" Catriona asked.

"Or had them killed. These men were left on MacDonell lands, so news of this was bound to make its way to me."

"Perhaps this is his way of proving to you that the men would meet justice?"

Liam shook his head in disgust. "If it is the man is truly unhinged."

"Gavin is not here," Catriona said.

"Who?"

"Macnaghten's illegitimate son. He is not here."

"It is unlikely that he would do something like this to his own son."

"Liam, I believe this may have been the work of his son."

He looked at her curiously, noticing the way thy her eyes were fascinated on the gaping wounds in his neck.

"What makes you say that?" he asked her.

"The night they found me. He slit the throat of one of the group members. Murdered him before my very eyes. I cannot picture Macnaghten doing something like this himself. But I have no problem believing that his son would do something this obscene."

"Come away now, love. There is nothing more we can do for them. Once we return to the keep I'll send men to cut the bodies down and see that the bodies are properly buried."

"It does not seem fair to leave them like this, even knowing all the horrible things they've done. It just seems wrong."

Liam leaned across his horse and took Catriona's reins, leading her mare away from the suspended bodies.

"I will take care of it, Catriona, I promise you. Try to put it out of your mind for now. Not much longer and we will be safely home."

Catriona nodded silently but did not respond, as they continued on down the path to Invergarry Castle.

CHAPTER 25

THE KEEP WAS BUZZING like a hive when Liam and Catriona finally made it back home. He was tired, dirty and weary, but the walls of Invergarry towering over him was one of the most beautiful sights he had ever seen.

"It's good to be home," he said as he helped Catriona down off of her horse.

"It will be wonderful to sleep in a proper bed again tonight. I hope to not have to travel for a very long time."

"Don't worry." A sly smile tugged at the corner of his mouth. "Now that I have you back home where ye belong, I've no plans on letting ye go wandering off for a very long time."

Catriona laughed and smiled up at him. "Well, ye have yourself a willing captive this time around, Laird MacDonell."

Liam laughed and bent low, kissing Catriona on the lips. The curve of her waist was warm and soft in his hands and he pulled her closer to him.

"Well now," came Iain's voice from behind them, "Isn't that a sight."

Catriona pulled away from Liam, and he enjoyed the pink flush that tinged her cheeks. Just the sight of it made him look forward to that night, when he hoped to make her flush all over.

"How are ye, brother?" he asked Iain.

"Very fine, though maybe not as fine as some, by the looks of the two of ye. I see ye've got yer lovely wife back home safe and in one piece."

"Aye, and there's much I need to tell ye, but first, how is Alex?"

"Why don't ye come see for yourself?"

"He's awake then?" Relief flooded Liam.

"Aye, and being a right terror on anyone who comes too close. At this rate it won't be long until we need to bind him to the bed. He keeps trying to get up even though the surgeon says he still needs much more bed rest."

"Well, Alex has never been one for sitting still."

Liam took Catriona's hand in his and the two of them followed Iain to Alex's bedchamber.

They found Alex propped up by pillows on his large bed, looking downright miserable.

"And where have you been?" Alex demanded when he saw his brother.

"Sorry Alex, there were a few things that I needed to handle."

Alex's eyes shifted to Catriona and his body stiffened. "What the hell is she doing here?" he asked glaring at her in disgust.

Liam felt Catriona cringe next to him as though Alex's words were a visible blow. She looked down at the floor, unable to meet Alex's accusing stare and pressed herself closer to Liam's side.

"Enough, Alex," Liam said. "Ye'll not be speaking to my

wife that way any longer. If ye have anything to say to her ye'll say it with a civil tongue in yer head."

"Yer wife, is it?" Alex scoffed. "Don't ye mean the enemy? One would almost think ye enjoy taking these serpents to yer bed, the way ye take to marrying vipers."

"Alex!" shouted Iain.

Alex groaned and shut his mouth, realizing that he had gone too far.

"What did ye say to me?" Liam said, coolly.

"Shit, Liam, I'm sorry. I had no call to say something so cruel to ye. But what the hell are ye doing with her, man? After everything her father has done?"

"It was not my father," Catriona said. Though her voice was low, it was steady, and she raised her head to meet Alex's accusations head on.

"I heard the cries myself? Are ye calling me a liar? That would be rich, coming from the little schemer that tricked my brother into marrying him."

Catriona squared her shoulders and strode over to Alex's bedside.

"I am not a liar," she said calmly. "My father is not innocent in this, I'll not make that claim. Yes, he did trick Liam into marrying me. I will admit to that as well. But I had no part in it. I was just as much a victim of my father's falsehood as Liam was. It was also not my father's men that attacked you nor burned down those homes. They were men hired by someone else entirely, set on framing my father."

Alex looked skeptical but sent a questioning glance in Liam's direction. Liam nodded but did not intervene, proud of Catriona for standing up for herself. Her father was right, while she may be gentle, she was in no way weak.

"I know that ye do not like me Alex, and ye do not trust me. But I am hoping, in time that I will come to call you brother and you see me as a sister. Liam can explain to you all that has happened in greater detail than I, and I am sure you are wanting some time alone with each other, so I will leave you in peace. But your brother and I have found a peace between us. I hope that you and I will find a similar peace."

Catriona turned her back on Alex without waiting for an answer and swept out of the room, pausing only long enough to reach out and squeeze Liam's hand as she passed by.

Liam watched his wife's regal exit from the chamber with no little amount of awe and pride. The thought of which would have made him laugh not long ago. But as he listened to the soft swishing of her skirts in the hall outside the door he could not stop himself from grinning.

"Is it as she says then?" Alex asked.

"It is," Liam said with a nod. "And so much more. Come Iain, find yourself a seat, for there is much I need to be telling ye both."

Catriona pressed a hand to her chest in a vain attempt to steady her pounding heart. She stood in Liam's bedchamber wearing only her shift and she shivered from the slight chill in the room. She felt wanton, standing in the middle of the chamber with her hair down and flowing around her shoulders, and beyond her nervousness was a deeper bubble of excitement.

The hour was late and he would be coming to bed soon, she could feel it. And when he did, she wanted him to find her there waiting for him. She had meant every word she said. She wanted them to move forward as husband and wife. And even as she tried to quell the nerves in the pit of her stomach, she knew without a doubt that she wanted to be with him tonight as man and wife in every sense. She wanted to give herself over to him completely.

Closing her eyes, she took a deep breath. This was what she wanted. And even though she could not completely quell the whisper of fear within her, she desperately wanted him to take her into his arms again. To feel the brush of his lips against her skin. The tingle of anticipation down her spine as he removed her clothing. The rolling desire crash over her once more as he pleasured her.

The seconds ticked by like hours as she waited for him to open the door.

Doubt began to nag at her as time passed with no sign of him, and she couldn't help but worry that she may have made a mistake by waiting for him here. He had so many things to see to, what if he was detained by some important clan business?

She bit her lip with worry and was considering heading back to her chamber when the door opened at last.

"Catriona?"

Liam paused in the doorway, surprised to see her standing there.

"I thought that I would join ye in here tonight. Unless ye would prefer to be alone?"

Liam's eyes flashed as he studied her and took a step further into the room, closing the chamber door behind him.

"I would love to have ye join me in here lass," he said, continuing to eye her form through her shift. "Have ye been here long?"

Taking a deep breath, Catriona took a step towards him and spoke with all the confidence that she could muster. "It felt like an eternity."

It only took Liam a few long strides to close the distance between them, and she gasped as her feet were suddenly no longer touching the ground.

She clutched at his shoulders, trying to find purchase as he carried her backwards in his arms, then suddenly her back collided roughly with the wall behind her. He pressed his body against hers, trapping her and holding her suspended in the air, before he kissed her hungrily. His teeth nipped at her bottom lip, and his tongue delved into her mouth, demanding a response.

She couldn't think. She could barely breathe as she kissed him back just as passionately. The need that raged in her felt unquenchable. Her hands ran through his hair, pulling his face closer, and she wrapped her legs more tightly around his waist, feeling the heat of his body through the thin material of her shift. But it was not enough, and her body screamed out for more.

Catriona groaned out loud at the illicit feeling of his tongue trailing down the long line of her neck and over her collarbone. Tilting her head back to allow him greater access as he dipped lower to her chest, she ground her pelvis against him, trying to satisfy the need she felt mounting there.

"God, Cat, ye're like fire in my hands," he panted.

A thrill went through her at his words. He had never called her Cat before, always Catriona. But there was something about hearing him say it now. It felt even more intimate than what they were doing to hear her name spoken like that on his lips.

His hands slid up her sides and grazed over her breasts. Catriona gasped as her nipples sharpened tightly in anticipation. Thankfully she didn't have long to wait for them to receive Liam's full attention.

Boosting her higher, he ran his tongue over one of her sensitive nipples, teasing it through the thin fabric. She arched her back, wanting more, but he refused to add more pressure.

With a deep satisfied chuckle, Liam abandoned her breast

to pay due attention to the other, teasing her second nipple with his tongue as he had the first.

"Why must you torture me?" Catriona gasped.

"Because yer body is begging to be tortured," he whispered into her breast before taking her nipple between his teeth and sucking on it hard.

She cried out and dug her nails into his shoulders, overcome by the pleasure that shot through her.

"More?" he asked her.

"Please. God, yes please," she gasped.

Gripping her tightly, Liam walked them over to the large bed, where he tipped her backwards, and gently lay her atop it.

She ran her hands down over the hard length of his muscular arms as he stood up straight and began to unbuckle his plaid. She watched him unwrap the long length of fabric and stared transfixed as it dropped to the floor. His eyes locked with hers as he took hold of his shirt and began to pull it up over his head.

Her heart pounded faster and her palms grew damp as more and more of his body was exposed. She was not sure if she would ever get used to the sight of seeing her husband naked.

She lay on the bed, propped up on her elbows, drinking in the sight of his broad muscular body, and her eyes widened at the sight of his manhood standing fully erect and at attention.

"Oh!"

Her eyes flew back to his, but she had to look away, her face burning.

"Are ye all right?" he asked her, his voice filled with concern.

He stepped closer and placed a hand gently on her lower leg. Slowly he slid it higher, trailing his fingers over the back of her knee, and then up over the outside of her thigh.

Catriona's skin broke out in gooseflesh at the whisper-light touch and she nodded, swallowing audibly.

"I just... I am not..."

"What is it?"

He leaned over, his exploring hand pushing the hem of her shift ever higher.

"You are... er... very large, are you not?" she stuttered. Her eyes flickered down to his manhood and then back up again.

"Dinna worry, Cat," he said, kissing her again. "I promise ye, it will fit."

She leaned forward and kissed him again, drawing him near, and he continued to raise her shift. She shuddered as the cool air hit her nether regions, but was soon distracted by his fingers brushing over her naked sex.

"Lift yer arms."

She did what he said without question, and he pulled the shift over her head and tossed it to the side. She was naked and completely exposed to him, but it felt wonderful to have his naked body pressed against hers.

"Ye're absolutely gorgeous, lass," he whispered in her ear.

"I want you" The words escaped her, unbidden, but they were the truth. She wanted him like she had never wanted any man before in her life.

"Make love to me, Liam. Make me your wife at last."

Liam pressed her back against the bed and began kissing her with more urgency. She abandoned herself to the feel of his touch as his eager hands flew over her body. He slipped one down between them and began stroking her sex, his deft fingers sliding along her slick folds, stoking her need. Using his thumb to put pressure on the sensitive bud, he slipped two of his fingers up inside of her and began thrusting in and out.

"Uh!" Catriona cried out as her hips matched his rhythm, and he began to thrust harder.

"Aye, Cat, purr for me," he demanded.

His hand kept the rhythm as he moved down her body, replacing the pressure of his thumb with the swirling, flicking motions of his tongue.

"Oh God, Liam... I cannot... I cannot take it!" Her whole body felt as though it were on fire as he pushed her closer to the edge.

"Aye, ye can and ye will."

She could feel herself teetering on the edge of a great release when suddenly his mouth and fingers were gone.

Catriona cried out in protest, but Liam was back on top of her in a flash, nudging her legs wider. She could feel herself stretching wider to accommodate him as he pressed the tip of his manhood into her virgin entrance.

"Liam," she moaned.

"Shhh, Cat, just kiss me."

He kissed her roughly, distracting her as he eased himself deeper. She had never felt so full and complete in her life. He began to move then, a slow steady rocking as he drew back and thrust into her again and again.

She brought her legs up and wrapped them around him, holding him tightly as she moved her hips to match his rhythm, urging him on.

She had never felt anything so glorious in her life, and the pleasure crested over her in waves. She gave her body up to the moment, riding her unbridled desire as they thrust harder and faster.

"God, Cat, I need ye. I need ye like I've never needed anyone before in my life," he groaned.

Catriona gripped him tighter and cried out as he rammed into her, the force of his desire pushing her over the edge and sending her spiraling as her body burst with pleasure. His roar of completion joined her own moments later, before he collapsed down on the bed beside her, panting for breath.

Catriona could barely feel her limbs. She felt weightless and blissfully happy. Liam's arm reached across her middle and hooked around her. He pulled her nearer to him, settling her snugly along his side.

"That was wonderful," she said wistfully, placing her hand tenderly on his chest. It rose and fell rapidly as he lay next to her, still recovering his breath.

"Aye, it was." He kissed the top of her head, and ran his hands slowly through her hair.

She closed her eyes and said nothing, sinking into the soothing touch of his gentle strokes.

"I never thought that I could feel this way with anyone," he said at last. His voice was barely above a whisper.

Catriona stayed silent. Afraid to break whatever spell had allowed him to open up to her.

"I never thought that I would know what it would be like to know happiness with a woman. To know peace with a wife. My wife. Thank ye, Catriona."

Her heart was so filled with joy she feared it would burst, and a silent tear rolled down her cheek, she was so moved by his words. She felt him press another light kiss to the back of her head, then she was soon met by the sound of his light snoring.

Catriona took Liam's hand and closed her eyes before instantly settling into a blissful sleep.

CHAPTER 26

CATRIONA HUMMED as she walked through the hallway, swaying slightly. Her heart was full, and she smiled to herself as her mind floated back to thoughts of the night before, and how wonderful it had felt to be held in Liam's arms. She had never experienced anything so incredible. Lost in her daydreams, she wasn't paying attention when a tall shadow crossed into her path.

"Easy there."

A male voice startled her out of her reverie, and she looked up to find Iain standing inner path.

"Good Lord," she said, holding a hand up to her chest where her heart was beating rapidly. "I swear it is becoming a habit with me of running straight into The MacDonell brothers in these halls."

Iain laughed and tucked her hand into the crook of his arm before continuing to accompany her down the hall. "By the sounds of it, if yer not more careful you'll be running us all down in due course."

Catriona laughed and patted her brother-in-law on the

arm. "I promise ye that I'll do my best to make sure that doesn't happen. I really should spend less time daydreaming."

"Ah, well now, I'm not so sure about that. Who doesn't enjoy daydreaming now and then?" He gave her a sly smile and crooked his eyebrow. "So, tell me Lady MacDonell, what is it that ye were dreaming about this morning?"

Catriona's face grew warm and she had no doubt that it was bright red from blushing. Embarrassed, she averted her eyes, unable to meet Iain's gaze.

"Ahhhh, so that's the way of it now, is it? Well, I'll admit that I'm glad to hear that you and my brother have come to see eye to eye at last."

"Iain!" Catriona gasped, shocked that he would suggest such things. She adored Iain and his easy smiles, but sometimes he really could be quite shocking.

Iain patted her hand in a soothing manner and pulled her into a small alcove just off the hall lowering his voice. "There is something that I've been meaning to say to ye, but with all the excitement, we have not had a chance to talk, you and I, one on one that is."

"What is it that ye wish to speak with me about?"

"I wanted to thank ye," he said simply.

"Thank me?" Catriona was confused. What could she have possibly done that Iain would want to thank her for?

"Yes. I want to thank you for helping Liam find some peace."

"Oh, Iain, I haven't done—"

"Yes, Catriona, ye have, whether ye know it or not. My brother is... well, we both know that he is not an easy man. He is stubborn, and can be the devil to deal with at times, but his heart has always been in the right place. He wants to be a good leader, and he has always been a good man. But for years that has been a restlessness in him, and a distrust. But ye, ye've opened him up. I saw it when he brought ye back after you left for yer father's. He told Alex and me the story of how Macnaghten took ye, and I tell ye, when he speaks to ye, the way he looks at ye. I have never seen him look at another that way before, not even Alana."

Catriona was touched by Iain's words. She wanted very much to believe that Liam cared for her in a way that he had never cared for another. She knew how much he had loved Alana, and she hoped that one day Liam would come to love her even more than he had loved his first wife,

"Do you love him?" Iain asked her.

Catriona was caught off guard by his question.

"I... well..."

"After all you've been through, I would understand if it were still a bit difficult for ye. But I want to believe that love is not out of the question."

"I do not, I mean, we have not. I do not know what ye want me to say. It feels... not right to speak of love with ye."

"If you feel it I would have ye say it. I would know that ye care. It would put my mind at ease."

Catriona looked at Iain and saw the pain and the worry in his eyes. The darker things that he spent his days hiding behind his jokes and laughter, and Catriona realized that Iain's carefree spirit was not so carefree as he wanted everyone to suppose.

Catriona placed a hand gently on his arm and looked him squarely in the eye. She had been uncomfortable speaking of love to Iain because she had not yet said the words to Liam himself. But now she could see that Iain cared for and wanted to protect his elder brother just had Alex had. He needed to know that Liam's heart was in careful hands at last.

"It is love that I feel." Catriona told him. "I know it is, and I could not deny it any more than I could hold back the waves of the sea. And I promise ye, that not another day will go by that my feelings can be called into question. It is love."

A large smile spread across Iain's face, and he gathered her up in his arms and spun her around in a circle. Setting her back down on the ground he grabbed her by the shoulders.

"Ye have no idea how happy that makes me to hear."

A sharp intake of breath drew their attention and Catriona and Iain turned to find Liam standing a few feet away, an indecipherable expression on his face.

"Liam," Catriona said. She moved to take a step toward him but was stopped by Iain's hands holding her fast. It was only then that she began to realize what it must have looked like to an observer, she and Iain huddled in the small alcove. "Liam, please."

Rage clouded over Liam's face, and he turned and walked away with speaking a word. "Liam, please wait!"

Iain dropped his hands, and Catriona took after Liam, praying that he would listen to reason.

Liam's mind swirled as he stumbled away from the scene he had just been witness to. "Is it love?" The words echoed again and again in his head, hammering at him from all sides.

Mere hours after his wife had given herself to him, she had declared her love for his brother. He could not banish the sight of them from his mind. The way they held onto each other with such ease. So much love filling her eyes.

The pain of their betrayal washed over him and swallowed him whole. He had given her his heart. He had opened up and poured into her all of the love and trust that he had within him. Determined to free himself from the chains of the past in order to make a future with her. But now, all he felt was a searing-hot rage. He loved her, and she loved his brother.

It was a though a rope were tightening around his throat, and his vision blurred. He saw nothing and no one as he put as much distance between the two lovers as possible, just heard the echoing voice of his brother, "Is it love?" as he held Liam's wife.

Once again he had fallen in love with a woman who made false promises to him all the while giving her heart to another. Was he destined to live his life as such a fool?

"Liam, please wait!"

Catriona's voice was a light humming in his ear, and he could barely make out her words or the sounds of her footsteps on the stones behind him.

"Liam!" Iain's voice called out to him, and his hands tightened into fists and his blood began to boil. His brother. His brother! Never in his life would he have believed that his own brother would be capable of such a betrayal.

A hand landed on his arm, and his haze broke. "Get off of me, ye bastard!" he roared. Tearing his arms out of Iain's grasp.

"Liam, ye must calm down," Iain said.

"Calm down, ye want me to calm down? I should run ye through where ye stand!"

"Dammit, man!" Iain looked around at the gathering crowd in the hallway and opened the nearest door before shoving his brother through it.

"If ye lay one more hand on me, Iain, I swear to God that I will cut them off!"

"Liam, ye must get ahold of yourself man! I know what ye think you saw, but I'll tell ye now that ye are terribly mistaken."

"Oh, mistaken am I?" Liam snorted. "Do ye take me for some kind of fool? A blind man could see what the two of ye were doing back there. And have ye so little care for me, that not only must ye woo my wife, but ye must do it out in the open for God and all to see?"

"I was not wooing yer wife!"

"Yer hands were all over her and ye were talking about love! I saw the way she touched ye. The way ye held her close. Do ye hate me so much? Do ye think me such of a fool that ye could make up any story ye pleased, and ye think that I would believe it?"

Liam rand a hand through his hair, agitated as he stormed back and forth, his thoughts swirling.

"Ye must think that I'm a born cuckold, the way that Alana played me for a fool. Ye could have any woman ye want, Iain ye always have. Why must it be MY WIFE! Could ye not see that I loved her? You who know me best? And ye would woo her anyway?"

"Liam, ye are not listening! Ye're seeing it all wrong!"

"I knew she preferred ye! She as much as said it from the start, but stupidly I believed her when she said she cared for me. That she wanted to start over and have a true marriage with me. And I allowed myself to believe it. But the truth is finally out she is just the same as Alana!"

"No, I am not!"

Liam had not even noticed that Catriona had entered the room. She had not said a word as he raged at his brother, but now that he saw her standing there, her eyes full of false tears and fear, fear at having being discovered for her false-ness at last, he wanted to strangle her.

"And you! Ye wee whore! Ye might think that ye had me fooled, but I see ye for who and what ye really are now."

Blinded by pain and betrayal, his words lashed out at her.

Catriona's eyes went wide with shock at his words.

"Ye will not speak to her that way!" Iain shouted.

"Aye, yes, come to yer trollop's defense. Well if ye want

my whore of a wife so badly, then you're more than welcome to her! And don't worry brother, she's only been used but the once."

Liam's face exploded with white-hot pain as Catriona's palm connected with it.

"You, Liam MacDonell, are a cruel, heartless bastard! You are the most stubbornly blind man I have ever met in my entire life. How DARE you say such absolutely horrid things about me! I regret the day I ever allowed myself to fall in love with you!"

Sobbing, Catriona turned on her heels and fled from the room.

"Right, then," said Iain. "Obviously ye aren't seeing sense so maybe this will help." Iain took two steps forward and then dived at his brother.

The two of them crashed into a small table and sent it flying as they crashed into the ground.

Though Liam outweighed him, Iain had always had the advantage of speed over his brother when catching Liam by surprise. His fists shot out fast while he had the upper hand, hitting his brother in the ribs and the jaw.

"Get the hell off of me!" Liam said, landing blow after blow of his own as he began to rapidly gain the upper hand.

"Not until you listen, you stupid, stubborn bastard."

"I'll not listen to more of yer lies," Liam shouted.

"Yes," Iain said, his voice low as he rolled, landing atop of Liam and pressing a sharp blade to his throat. "You will."

Liam eyed his brother coolly as the sharp steel bit into his skin. "You would kill me for her then?"

"Listen to me Liam, and listen to me well. I am not in love with Catriona, nor she with me. What ye saw between us in that alcove was the two of us discussing her love for you. I was asking her if she loved ye. And she told me yes. I hugged her because I was happy for the two of ye. Happy that ye had a chance for peace at last. I've been worried about ye since the death of Alana, and in that moment I believed that I needn't worry about ye any longer, now that the two of ye had found each other."

Iain removed the blade from Liam's neck and slid it back into his sheath.

"But I cannot be sure if the damage ye've just done can ever be repaired." Iain got up off of his brother and walked out of the room, leaving Liam bruised and sore on the floor by himself to consider in horror the magnitude of the mistake he had just made.

Liam stared after his brother as Iain's words sunk in, and as the truth of his admission registered, Liam's blood ran cold at the fear of the irreparable damage he may have just done. There was no way that Catriona could possibly forgive him now, and whatever love she felt for him had probably just been destroyed forever.

CHAPTER 27

CATRIONA RUSHED out into the darkness, unable to see even a few short feet in front of her, blinded by the tears that flooded her eyes. How could Liam accuse her of such things after all that they had been through? She had tried to show him how much she cared for him. That she had grown to love him. Yet his faith in her was still not strong enough to quell the suspicion voice in his heart.

Catriona tripped on a rock and let out a yelp as she fell forward onto her knees in the dirt. Her hands stung as they scraped across the dirt and rocks, and she clutched her torn, bleeding hands to her chest.

"Damn that Alana!" she shouted into the night. Curse her for the damage that she had done. The damage that she continued to do. Why must Catriona be the one to pay for the selfish woman's sins? She had never met her, and yet it was as though Alana had vowed to plague Catriona's life and destroy any hope she may have for happiness from beyond the grave.

If Liam himself could not move past the pain that his first wife had brought upon him, how could Catriona ever hope to hold a place in his heart? With all of the sorrow and suspicion that it had been filled with, she was losing hope that there was any room within it for him to love her.

She took a deep hiccupping breath and raised a hand to her face to wipe away the hot trail of tears when she heard light footsteps coming from behind her.

"Just leave me be," she sobbed. But as she turned to face whoever had approached her, an arm wrapped around her and a large hand was clasped over her mouth.

Terror flooded Catriona's body as the memory of being taken by the reavers came rushing back.

"How very nice to see ye again, Lady MacDonell," a voice hissed into her ear. "I've missed ye very much."

Catriona struggled furiously to break out of the man's grip. She would have known that voice anywhere, there was no chance of her forgetting it until the day she died. Gavin.

"Now, now," he said wrapping his other hand around her throat and squeezing it tightly. "Calm yourself. If ye make too much noise and alert anyone to my presence, well, I would be forced to kill them. And you wouldn't want to have their deaths on your conscience, now, would ye?"

Spots were starting to form in front of her eyes, and her head began to spin, but Catriona was able to nod her head ever so slightly.

"Good, that's very good. Very smart." Gavin released the grip on her throat and Catriona slumped in his grip, sucking in deep gasps of air.

"Now then, the two of us are going to go for a little walk."

"I'm not going anywhere with you!" Catriona hissed.

"Yes," he said, spinning her around to face him. Catriona stared deep into the black pits of his eyes. Eyes she had prayed to never have to be face-to-face with again and cringed. "Ye are." He moved quickly, too quickly for her to move out of his way. Grabbing her by a handful of hair he slammed her head into the stone wall of the keep. A loud crack echoed in her ears and then the world around her faded to black.

The floor was cold and hard beneath Catriona's bruised aching body. She groaned lightly and slowly cracked her eyes open. The light was dim in the small room but as she strained to look around she saw Gavin sitting on a stool in a corner staring at her with disgust in his eyes.

"So ye're awake then. I was starting to get impatient."

Catriona tried to sit up but found her hands and feet bound. "Where..." she tried to speak but her throat was sore and raw and her head throbbed from where it had hit the wall with enough force to knock her unconscious. Closing her eyes, she took a deep breath and tried to speak once more. "Where am I?" She asked him.

"I've brought you someplace very special. Someplace that was just for me and the woman I loved."

Catriona's eyes opened wide. It was impossible to believe that this man, this horrible human being had ever been capable of loving another person. She found it highly doubtful that he would know what love was.

"Loved?" Catriona asked, wondering what had happened to the woman.

"Yes, 'loved,' and love. I still love her even though I can no longer be with her. She is now forever out of my reach."

Catriona felt nothing but relief for whoever the poor woman was that had somehow been saved by Gavin's affections. She could not imagine how horrifying it must have been to know that you were the object of Gavin's love.

"What happened to her?" She asked him.

Gavin's eyes had a faraway look, and he was no longer

looking at Catriona, but through her, past her, as though her were seeing something completely different from the dingy little room.

"She was the most beautiful girl I had ever seen," he said, his voice wistful as he remembered back to the day he first laid eyes on the woman he loved.

"I was with my father. We had ridden down to the village together and he knocked on the door of a hut and a beautiful woman answered the door. She had long black hair all the way down her back and large, striking green eyes. I remember being shocked when we stepped inside her home, and my father kissed her on the lips. I had no clue who the woman was, my father had never mentioned her before.

"She led him upstairs, and I sat in the small parlor waiting for him to come back down when the front door opened again, and a gorgeous young woman walked in. She was the spitting image of her mother. Long black hair and the same large emerald-green eyes. She was surprised to see me sitting there all alone but when she heard the noises from upstairs all she did was cock her head and ask, 'He's here again isn't he?' It was then I realized that whoever the woman was, my father had been visiting her for some time. She led me outside, away from the noise of our parents upstairs, and we sat together on the low stone wall that encircled her house. What we talked about, I can barely remember, I just remember being so entranced by her. By the way she looked, and moved, the way she laughed. She was so full of life. I wanted her.

"My father took me with him to the village many times after that, giving the girl and me plenty of time to get to know each other. I don't know how it happened. I don't know if it was just because she was as lonely as I. But in time, she came to love me. We only had each other. Our trysts coincided with those of our parents, taking the time we found alone to spend with one another. I promised her that I would marry her one day. But then the worst happened.

"One day I went to visit her and when I arrived at the door, she would not see me. It was clear to see that she had been crying. After much begging, she finally admitted to me that she was to be wed. Her mother had made her an advantageous match, and there was nothing that could be done to change it.

"I told her that I would go to her mother and tell her that I wanted to marry her daughter. I could ask my father to intercede on my behalf. But she said that it would do no good. That her mother would never allow her to marry the unacknowledged bastard of her lover.

"But I told her that we could not go without a fight. So I went to her mother and proclaimed my love for her daughter, and I swore that I would take care of her for the rest of her life. Her face. I cannot explain to you the expression of sorrow that passed over her mother's face with every word I said.

"'Is what he says true?' she demanded of her daughter. And when my love confirmed my words she lashed out and slapped her with such force that she was knocked into the table and fell to the ground. She hit the edge of the table with such force that she miscarried and lost the baby that I did not know she was carrying.

"Her mother wept, but not at the loss of her unborn grandchild. She declared our baby an abomination. Created out of an unnatural love. An evil love. It was then we learned that we were half-brother and -sister. In all the years that my father had been visiting her mother, neither of us had known that he was her father as well. She had known a father growing up. He was a baker in the village, and a wonderful father from the stories she had told me. But it turned out that she, like me, was another of my fathers unclaimed bastards.

"There was no way for us to be wed. Her condition was hidden from her intended until she could recover, and then, not long after, she was wed to her loathsome husband, the damnable Laird MacDonell."

Catriona listened to his story, her eyes wide with horror, and even as he described the unspeakable love that he and his half-sister shared, she could not say that she was completely surprised to discover that the woman he first loved was Alana.

"Even as my love and Liam were married, we continued to see one another. She refused to bed him, you see," a self-satisfied smirk ghosted across Gavin's face. "She kept herself only for me, for she was disgusted by the very thought of his touch. It was me she loved, and no other. And then one night, when she was on her way to see me, her horse threw her and she broke her neck." Gavin turned to Catriona, his face twisted in a mask of rage. "If only she had been free to marry me. We could have gone away together. Started a new life where no one knew who we were. Her parentage was already a secret, we could have lived a happy life if it wasn't for her selfish whore of a mother!"

He lurched out of the chair and swept an arm across the table, sending the items upon it flying across the room. "It's MacDonell's fault she is dead! And I will not allow him happiness with another. I will not allow him to forget what he did to my Alana!"

Catriona shrank back as Gavin stormed across the room and grabbed her roughly by the hair on the top of her head. "Maybe I will send you back to him with her name carved across that pretty face of yours," he hissed. "Let you be a constant reminder of her whenever he looks at you? Would you like that? Would you like to be my messenger?"

The violent blow landed on her cheek, and her face

exploded in pain where his fist landed. She raised her hands to fend him off but he reared back and struck her once more.

Catriona went sprawling and tried in vain to crawl away but he was soon atop her.

"Get off me!" she screamed as he roughly flipped her over onto her back. "Get off!"

"That's right, scream for me, ye wee bitch!" Gavin straddled her and wrapped his hands around her neck. Catriona clawed at him, raking her nails across the back of his hands as she tried to pry them off of her throat, but she was not strong enough. His gripped tightened and she kicked out, her legs flailing, her body desperate for air.

Gavin's face loomed close as he continued to choke her, a manic smile spread across his face, his black eyes shining as they bore into her.

Her eyes watered and the edges of her vision began to blur and disappear.

"Let's see how that MacDonell bastard handles having two dead wives on his hands."

Catriona's arms fell to her sides, the last of her strength gone, and her eyes fluttered shut on Gavin's twisted face.

CHAPTER 28

LIAM HAD SEARCHED the keep from top to bottom and there was still no sign of Catriona anywhere. A kernel of fear settled in the pit of Liam's stomach. What if he couldn't find Catriona in the keep because she was no longer there? What if he had finally succeeded in driving her off? She could be somewhere hiding from him, or even worse, on her way back to her father's house already. And could he blame her? Once again he had failed her. At the first opportunity to show her that he had changed, that she could trust him, he instead turned on her yet again.

It pained him to look back and remember the hurt he saw in her eyes when he had accused her of desiring his brother. Her shock when he had called her a whore. His words had been inexcusable. He wanted to vomit from the shame of his actions. He didn't deserve her. She was too kind, too open, too loving, and too precious. Just being near her filled him with hope and light. He could no longer deny that that was why he had pulled away from her for so long. He had been too afraid of the things she made him feel. He would give anything, anything, for the chance to tell her that he loved her and have her know it to be true.

"Liam." He turned at the sound of Iain's voice.

"Have ye found her?" he asked.

"I've seen no sign of her."

"Do ye think she would have... Do ye think she may have...?"

"What?" Iain asked.

"Left me." Liam forced out through clenched teeth.

Iain could not meet his eye and that was all the answer Liam needed.

There was a shouting coming from downstairs that drew Liam's attention from his thoughts. He exchanged a look with his brother.

"What on earth is that?"

"I dinna know," said Iain, a worried expression on his face.

"You dinna think that something could have happened to Catriona? Maybe someone has found her injured somewhere?"

Liam took off down the hallway, leaving his brother to follow behind. When he reached the main floor in front of the great hall he saw his brother Alex standing with Laird Macnaghten trying to hold him back. Macnaghten struggled against the two men that held him, and shouted for Liam, a piece of paper clenched in his fist.

"I must see Laird MacDonell, there is no time to waste. I demand that ye unhand me man!" Macnaghten cursed them.

"Alex, what is going on here?" Liam asked.

"I do not know, Liam, the man will not say, he just came in here demanding to see ye."

"What is it that I can do for ye, Laird Macnaghten?" Liam asked him. The sight of the man filled him with disgust. He could still picture the five men that Macnaghten had sentenced to die in the back of his mind. Had he ordered his son to stake them out on the edge of his lands as well? He was well and truly finished with any dealings with the man.

"Not here," Macnaghten said, casting a glance around the room at the crowd his entrance had drawn. "I must talk to ye in private and we have no time to waste."

"Whatever ye need to say to me ye can say it here," said Liam, not unsure that the man may try an attempt on his life if he was alone in a room with him. He was not sure if Macnaghten had truly given up the belief that Liam was the cause of Alana's death.

"It must be in private MacDonell, it must!" Laird Macnaghten lowered his voice and leaned forward. "It is about Gavin. I fear ye and yer wife are in great danger."

Liam's heart dropped. "Release him," he told his brother and the other man. "Come with me." he told Macnaghten and led him into the great hall. "Everybody out!" Liam's shout rang out across the room, and though the command raised a few eyebrows, the few people that were inside the great hall got up to leave casting curious expressions his way.

"Now Macnaghten, we are alone. Tell me what you have to tell me about Gavin and be quick about it."

"I went to speak to Gavin, about the dispatching of the reavers. I wanted to make sure that he had delivered them into yer hands for justice. I thought that it would be a good way to make peace between us. If the reavers saw justice at yer hands ye would know that I intended to keep my word about dropping my grudge against ye. But Gavin did not return from the task I sent him. Days went by and he did not return nor send word of why he was delayed. Then I received the letter ye sent me, telling me of the bodies of the reavers ye found at the edge of yer land. I tell ye this now

MacDonell, I did not order my son to do that. I never would have ordered him to do such a thing."

"But ye would order him to burn my villagers' homes to the ground?"

"I was crazed with grief, MacDonell, and I wanted ye to suffer. But destroying homes is not the same as murder, and ye ken that just as well as I do."

"Yer men murdered the people that lived in those homes as well."

"Again I tell ye that that was not at my word. But none of this matters, MacDonell! Not at this moment. What has been done cannot be undone. What matters is what I found later!"

"And what is that?" Liam asked him, crossing his arms over his chest.

"Gavin left me a letter when he set out to bring ye the band of reavers. I somehow missed it as it was buried under some papers I put atop my desk. "

"And what did this letter say?"

"It said that Gavin planned on doing what I obviously did not have the courage to do myself, and that was deal with ye properly. He said that he knew in his heart that ye were the blame of Alana's death and he would see to it that yer life was destroyed for it, if it was the last thing he did."

"Gavin knew Alana?"

"Yes! They knew each other when they were younger. I sometimes brought him with me when I went to the village to visit Alana's mother and that is how they met."

"Did they ken that they were half-brother and -sister?"

The blood drained out of Macnaghten's face. "No, and God help me for that, because it could have saved all of us so much pain. I went to search his rooms to see if there was anything there that would help me to discover his plan, and that's where I found these." Macnaghten held out the piece of paper he was holding. "There were more of them, many, many more."

"What is it?" Liam asked.

"It is a letter, from Alana to her brother. I do not think you want to read it. It is..." Macnaghten closed his eyes and hung his head in shame. "I had no idea, MacDonell, I promise ye that. I swear it to ye. I had no idea that the two of them were... I did not even know that they kept in contact. But I sent my son on many missions for me. Errands that took him all over the highlands. And God help me, but the letters claim that the two of them were in love."

Shock rolled through Liam as though he had been struck by a fist directly in the face and nausea rolled though him. "What?" He let out a strangled cry.

"Alana was sneaking off to see a lover. It was her half-brother. They were in love long before she agreed to marry you. And they spoke of... I am so sorry MacDonell, but they spoke of a child that had been lost. Their child."

Liam felt his knees go weak, he could not believe the words he was hearing. His first wife had been in love with her brother all along. Had gotten pregnant by him? And even after she and Liam were wed, had continued to sneak out to see him? He could hardly credit such a thing.

"You are certain of this?" Liam demanded. "Absolutely certain?"

"I am. It was all there in the letters. But there were also directions to a place not far from here, where they used to meet for their dalliances. I do not know what Gavin could be planning against you, but there is a fair chance he could be hiding there while he comes up with his scheme."

Fear rocked Liam to the core as his wife came to his mind. "Catriona!"

"What?"

"I have been unable to find Catriona for hours. If this

place is not far from here, there is a chance that your son has my wife!"

"God help her," Macnaghten gasped. "I do not want to imagine what he could do to her in his state of mind."

"If he has harmed her, I promise ye, I will tear yer son limb from limb with my bare hands."

CHAPTER 29

THE TREES WHIPPED past and Liam pushed his stallion to its limit as he and Laird Macnaghten raced up the lane to the small house where Gavin and Alana used to meet in secret. The small house was only an hour's ride from Invergarry.

The windows of the small home were all dark, save for a dim orange glow that he could make out in one of the upstairs windows, beckoning them closer. Taunting them in the night.

He pulled hard on the reins, bringing his horse to a harsh stop, then jumped down, following close on Macnaghten's heels. Rage burned within him and he flexed his fingers, itching to wrap them around Gavin's neck for daring to lay hands on his wife.

"Hold fast, MacDonell," Macnaghten whispered as Liam reached for the door to the small house.

"We dinna have time for this, Macnaghten. If ye do not think ye can face yer son, ye dinna need to worry. I will happily deal with him for ye."

Macnaghten shook his head and grasped Liam's arm firmly. "That is not what I mean. Gavin is not right in the head, and I've no idea what he might do. If ye go bursting in there, there's no telling what he may do to yer wife. We have to be smart about this. Let me go in there first. Maybe I can reason with him."

"Do ye really think that yer son is someone that can be reasoned with? Nay. I'll not let ye go in there and waste what precious little time we may have. Ye can go in first, but I'll be right behind ye. Maybe we can catch him off guard and get Catriona to safety."

Macnaghten hesitated for a moment, then jerked his head in a sharp nod. "Aye, that may work. Give me a couple of minutes, then follow behind me."

Liam released the door handle and took a step back. Every instinct in his body urged him to go crashing through that door, but Macnaghten had a point. Startling a man like Gavin could set him off, and there was no telling what he may do if he felt cornered. He desperately wanted to get to Catriona, but caution was going to have to be the way of things.

Macnaghten took hold of the door handle in his place and held Liam's gaze before giving a silent nod and opening the door as quietly as possible. The door opened into a darkened room and Liam watched Macnaghten step into the silent room when suddenly something moved quickly in the dark and the older man cried out as he went crashing to his knees on the floor, holding the back of his head in his hands.

Liam froze for a moment, caught off guard by the sudden attack, quickly recovered as he stared into the shadowed face of a man standing over Macnaghten, a candlestick held high in the attacker's hand. Gavin.

With a roar, Liam dove through the door and tackled Gavin to the ground, the both of them crashing into a small table on the way down.

"Gavin!" Macnaghten cried out as he struggled to his feet. "Gavin, enough of this!"

Liam and Gavin grappled on the floor of the house, and Liam's fist swung out, connecting with Gavin's face, even as Gavin wrapped his hands around Liam's throat.

Using as much leverage as he could, Liam rolled them over once more so that he had the upper hand, but he could not loosen the grip around his throat. As he stared into the empty black depths of Gavin's eyes, he reached for the sgian dubh that was tucked into the top of his sock. Grasping the small blade, he brought it up and stabbed it into Gavin's side.

"Arg!" Gavin cried out and grabbed onto the hand Liam still had wrapped around the hilt of his blade as he held it fast in Gavin's side.

Taking advantage of Gavin's weakened grip he brought his head down as hard as possible onto Gavin's face, and twisted the knife in his side at the same time. Gavin released him at last as he cried out in pain and Liam reared back and sent his fist crashing down in Gavin's face with all of his strength.

"Where is she?" he yelled and he brought his fist down on Gavin over and over again. "Where is my wife!"

Liam could barely see for his rage and grabbed Gavin by the shirt front and hauled him up off the floor that was rapidly being stained by the blood from the wound in Gavin's side.

"If ye dinna tell me where my wife is, I swear to ye I will let ye bleed out on this floor, and there is not a soul in this world that would mourn ye. Now where is my wife!"

Gavin's eyes flicked to the staircase and Liam released him roughly. He stumbled towards the staircase praying that he would find Catriona safe upstairs. With each step he climbed a pit of fear grew in his stomach until he thought that he would buckle beneath the weight of it. It was a short hallway, and there was a soft glowing light under the crack of the door to his left at the top of the stairs. He pushed open the door and a strangled whimper tore out of him as he found Catriona lying motionless on the floor of the small bedroom.

"Catriona!" He collapsed next to her and gathered her head in his hands. "Catriona! Wake up, lass." Still she did not respond, and he ran his hand over her body, searching for a heartbeat, trying to quell the rising panic that threatened to consume him. "Don't be dead," he begged. "Please, lass, dinna be dead."

Deep red fingermarks marred the ivory skin of her throat, and he had to fight the urge to leave her there in order to return downstairs and finish what he had started with Gavin.

He pressed his fingertips to her as gently as possible, not wanting to do her any more harm. Finally, he was able to feel the faintest of beats in her throat, and he gathered her pale body to him as he shook with relief.

He picked Catriona up and carried her back downstairs as gently as he could. Catriona's light body was the most precious package he had ever had charge of. As he descended the stairs, he saw Macnaghten by Gavin's side, attempting to staunch the flow of blood from the wound Liam had inflicted.

Laird Macnaghten took a look at Catriona's motionless body, and his round face went pale in the dim light that flooded into the room from the open door. "Is she alive?" he asked Liam.

"Just barely." He looked down at Gavin who was watching him through the thin slit in one of his bloody, swollen eyes, the other too battered to open at all. Liam fought the urge to finish what he had started. But now that he had Catriona back, getting her medical attention was more important than exacting his revenge, no matter how tempting the thought.

"I'll leave ye to see that justice is done," Liam said to Macnaghten.

"Better to finish me off, MacDonell," Gavin choked out in raspy laugh. "Because if I dinna die here, I promise ye. I will find a way to make ye and yer whore wife pay. This is not the end."

Sorrow clouded Laird Macnaghten's face as he stared down at the monster that his son had become.

Liam placed Catriona gently on the table and pressed his lips lightly to her forehead. Taking his knife in hand again, he turned and knelt down next to Gavin across from Laird Macnaghten, not taking his eyes off of Gavin's father. Macnaghten gave an almost imperceptible nod of his head and looked away as Liam leaned over his son, unable to meet Liam's gaze.

Liam pressed the edge of his blade to Gavin's throat as he stared down into his battered face. He would do whatever it took to protect Catriona from Gavin's madness. His wife may never forgive him for the pain he had caused her, but he would make damn sure that she would never have to worry about Gavin again.

"If ye see Alana in the afterlife, tell her I hope she finally found peace." He slit Gavin's throat without hesitation.

Gavin lifted his hands weakly to his throat, and Liam watched numbly as the blood seeped out from between his fingers.

Turning, he gathered up Catriona without a word to Macnaghten, who continued to sit in silence on the floor next to the lifeless body of his broken son, left alone with the ghosts of his children to haunt him.

Liam sat at Catriona's bedside as she lay unmoving in her bed. She had been placed back in her old bedchamber at Invergarry Castle so that she could recover in peace.

He held one of her delicate hands in both of his, marveling at how small and frail it looked. Her skin was cool to the touch and unnaturally pale, but for the dark circles beneath her eyes, and the bruising that had darkened on her cheek and temple from where Gavin had struck her.

Three days had passed since he had found her. Three long days where she lay there, unmoving, unresponsive to his pleas, promises, and prayers. He would give anything for her to come back to him. He would even make a deal with the devil himself if that's what it took to make Catriona open her eyes once more.

"She still has not moved?"

Liam looked up into the worried face of his brother Alex and shook his head. "No, not yet."

"Ye should get some rest. Real rest. In your own bed. I can watch over her for ye if ye like, while ye're sleeping."

Liam shook his head and turned away from his brother, back to where Catriona lay. "Nay, I'll not leave her side. What if she were to awaken, and I was not here?"

"If she wakes up, I will send someone to fetch ye straight away, but ye cannot stay here forever. Ye need to get some rest. Have ye slept at all?"

"A little, here and there. It matters not. Ye'll not convince me to go. When she awakens, I want my face to be the first face she sees. I want her to know that I never left her. That I never left her side. And then maybe, just maybe she'll believe me when I tell her how sorry I am. That I know what happened to her was all my fault." His hands curled into fists, his fingernails digging into the palms of his hands, and he gazed down into her pale face. Somehow, even broken and bruised she was gorgeous beyond belief, and he knew that every scratch, bruise, and mark on her fair skin was because of him.

It did not matter what it took. He would spend every day of the rest of his life making it up to her.

Alex laid a hand on his brother's shoulder and squeezed gently. "What happened to her was not your fault."

Liam brushed Alex's hand away, not wanting to be comforted. Not wanting to be relieved of the guilt that gnawed away at his innards. "Aye, Alex, it is. If it weren't for me she never would have run off. She never would have been taken."

"The only one to blame for what happened to her is that bastard Gavin, and ye made sure that he would never be able to hurt her again."

"Aye, but the damage was already done. And now, just look at her. What if she does not wake up? What if she is not strong enough? Another wife, dead. But this time I truly would be to blame."

Deep lines formed on Alex's brow as he stared down at his eldest brother. "I should have been more kind to her," he said at last.

"What?" Liam looked back up again, confused.

"I should have been more kind to her. I did not trust her. I did not believe she loved ye, and I did not think she belonged here. I was rude to her. I did not make her feel welcome, and I did nothing to hide my dislike of her. Maybe if I had welcomed her into our home instead of treating her so poorly she would not have felt so alone. Maybe she would not have run off as she did."

"That's absurd," Liam said, dismissing the idea.

"Why would I be any less to blame than you? The only one of us that truly welcomed her into this family was Iain. He was the only one of us not to let her down. At least you saved her. You brought her back here. But what have I done?"

"Bringing her back was not your responsibility."

"Maybe not. But ye love her. And I promise ye that when she wakes up, and I tell ye Liam, that she will wake up. I will treat her as I would my own beloved sister. I swear it to ye. She will never doubt that this is where her home is. That this is where she belongs."

Liam squeezed his eyes shut and held his wife's small hand tightly, breathing deeply to hold back the tears that now burned at his eyes.

"She will wake up. She has to."

"She will, Liam. Dinna lose faith."

CHAPTER 30

SHE WAS DROWNING. Terror enveloped her as Gavin's cruel face formed in her mind. His large hands reached out to her, cutting through inky darkness where she floated. She opened her mouth to scream for help, but no sound escaped as his hands wrapped themselves around her, his fingers searing her skin as they made contact. He held her tightly, determined to drag her back down into the bottomless inky pit.

She struggled against him, lashing out to free herself, and fought toward the surface of her mind. Desperate to escape the hold that he had on her. She did not know where she was or how long she had been there, but she knew that she could not stay. She had to get back. To where? She did not know. She could not remember. But she knew that the longer she dwelled in that never-ending darkness, the more dangerous it would become, and she may never find her way home. She had to keep fighting. She had to get back...

Every inch of her body ached and she winced at the dull throbbing in her head. Catriona struggled to open her heavy eyelids, but when they finally cracked open the light in the room burned her eyes. She turned her head away to shield herself from the light of the candles burning next to her bed. But it was not Gavin's angry face that greeted her.

Liam sat slouched in a chair next to the bed in which she lay, his arms crossed over his chest, which rose and fell with each deep breath he took. His soft rhythmic snoring was oddly comforting.

She struggled to sit up, and let out a soft groan as her aching muscles protested her movements.

"Wha—?" Liam jerked awake, startled by the sound coming from the bed. His eyes locked with Catriona's and Catriona began to shake.

As she stared into his eyes she suddenly remembered the last words he spoke to her. All relief at Gavin's absence was swept aside, scattered like leaves to be replaced by the pain of Liam's accusations.

"Ye're awake," Liam whispered, sitting up straighter in his chair. "Oh, my God, ye're awake."

Liam grabbed her by the hand and brought it to his lips, covering every inch of it in fevered kisses.

"I thought I was going to lose ye," he whispered into her palm.

She sat frozen with shock as a tear rolled down his cheek and landed on her finger.

"I…" The word came out as a raspy croak. She winced and stopped. Her throat was raw and tender, making it painful to speak.

"Shhh, lass. Save yer strength." Liam rose from his chair and sat by her side on the edge of her bed. He reached out to her, his hand hovering just out a few inches from her throat and his face clouded over in anger.

"He did that to ye."

It was not a question. Catriona nodded and raised her hand to the dark purple bruises that Gavin had left on her skin.

"Oh God, Cat. Can ye ever forgive me? I ken I have no right to ask it of ye. I know what I said to ye, the way I've treated ye is beyond forgiveness." His voice broke and his entire body shook as he clutched at the bed coverings. "But I beg ye, I beg ye to give me one final chance to show ye that I can be worthy of ye."

Catriona shook her head and turned her face away from him as tears rolled down her cheeks. She had heard it all before. How could she trust that he meant it this time? How could she entrust her heart to him again after he had broken it so completely by believing she would deceive him with Iain?

"Please, Cat. Please don't turn away from me," he begged. "I can never make right the things I said, and I would understand if ye want nothing more than to see me dead on the floor before ye. But I tell ye this now, I will work every day for the rest of our lives to bring ye nothing but happiness. I would have given my life for yers if he had demanded it of me if it meant that ye would have been safe."

He grasped her hands in his and held them to his heart. Catriona could feel the rapid beat pounding in his chest as he bent his head to their joined hands.

"Ask it of me and it is yers. Anything. There is nothing too great. All that I have, and all that I am is yers."

She inhaled sharply as he raised his head and stared at her, unprepared for the fierceness of his gaze.

"I love ye, Catriona. I love ye with every last part of me. I should have told ye sooner. I should not have been such a coward, and a coward I was. But never again."

Catriona bit her lip as she studied him. Pain warred with hope within her as she listened to his words.

He loved her.

She had been aching to hear those words from his lips for

weeks. And now that he had finally said them, she desperately wanted to believe they were true.

"Please, Catriona, I beg of ye. If ye love me, don't let go."

Catriona, choked out a sob and wrenched her hands out of Liam's, only to quickly throw herself forward and wrap her arms around her neck, heedless of the pain.

The room tilted and swayed around her, and for a brief moment she feared she may lose consciousness once more. But she knew in her heart that if she did, she was safe at last in Liam's arms. He loved her.

"I thought I had lost ye." He whispered into her hair. His strangled voice was choked with unshed tears. "I was so afraid that ye would not wake up again. When I found ye laying there after what he had done to ye. Oh God, Cat, I have never been so afraid in my entire life. But I promise ye, ye never have to be afraid of him again. He's gone now, and never coming back."

Catriona pulled back from him and looked around the room. Only now fully realizing that she was back in her bedchamber.

"You... came... for... me...?" she said slowly, struggling with every word.

"Aye lass, I came for ye. I would have given my life for ye."

She closed her eyes as he gently brushed the hair away from her face.

Hope rose within her at the feel of his gentle fingertips across her sensitive skin, and she knew that no matter what may have come between them before, her heart belonged to him and him alone.

And as she opened her eyes to gaze into his, she saw the same love and need echoed back at her from within him.

Catriona raised her hand to Liam's cheek and smiled.

"I... love... you... too..."

EPILOGUE

The Highlands, Scotland
  Early Summer, 1620

The gentle ripples on the surface of Lock Oich glittered in the afternoon sun, and Catriona inhaled deeply, savoring the rich deep scent of grass and dirt that was still slightly damp from the rain the night before. A breeze cut through the glen, tossing her hair across her face, and she smiled, brushing it away gently.

"Ye're meant to be holding still," Liam told her, though he did not look up from the large sheet of paper he was sketching on.

"I am holding still." She laughed, as the wind tousled her hair again, and once more she brushed it away from her face.

Liam looked up and raised an eyebrow at her. "Ye call that holding still, do ye?"

"It's not my fault that it's so windy out here today. I'm holding mostly still. If I remember correctly, it was you that insisted my hair be loose."

"Aye well, ye look lovely with it down around yer shoulders like that."

Her body flushed warmly as his eyes trailed down over her curves and then back up to hold her gaze. She was still getting used to the way he complimented her so readily, and the look of desire that flashed in his eyes when he looked at her. A desire that she felt echoing inside her, making her want to reach out for him and have him take her up in his arms.

She blushed and looked away, breaking their eye contact, but a smile touched her lips.

"Do ye think..." she cleared her throat gently and looked back at him once more. "Do ye think that our children will have an affinity for drawing?"

"Our children?" His brow furrowed.

"Yes." She nodded and placed a hand gently on her stomach, to the secret she held there, a wide grin spreading across her face. "Our children."

"Catriona, are ye...? Are ye telling me that ye're...?"

She nodded her head enthusiastically and a laugh burst forth from her chest. She had not known when the best time would be to tell him, but she could not hold it back for any longer. "Yes! Yes, yes I do believe I am."

Liam let out a whoop and tossed his sketch pad aside, knocking over his container of charcoals and paints as he dove towards his wife and gathered her into his arms.

"Oh!" Catriona let out in a gush of air as he landed squarely on top of her and covered her face in frantic kisses.

"Ye're pregnant?"

"I am."

"Ye're pregnant!"

"I am!" she shouted with a laugh.

He placed his hand on her stomach and let it rest there,

imagining the tiny child that was even now growing inside of his wife. "Our own wee bairn," he whispered.

He gazed deep into her eyes with such love and tenderness that Catriona felt so overwhelmed tears began to well up in her eyes.

She wrapped her arm around him and pressed a kiss to his lips, filling it with all of the joy that she felt.

"Aye," he said, pulling back from her slightly. "Aye, I think they will love to paint. And we'll bring them here, to the banks of Loch Oich. And I'll tell them the story of how I was staring into their mother's eyes, eyes as blue as the loch itself, when she told me she was pregnant, and gave me the greatest gift of all."

THANK YOU FOR READING

I hope that you enjoyed this book. Keep watching my website to find more of my work, and don't forget to sign up for my newsletter in order to find out about new releases and get access to exclusive stories! If you enjoyed this book, please consider taking a moment to leave a review. Thank you.

- Stephanie

Website

www.StephanieMarksBooks.com

Newsletter

Sign me up!

ALSO BY STEPHANIE MARKS

~THE VANESSA KENSLEY SERIES~

BLOOD AND HUNGER

SANGUINE MOON

~THE CLAN MACGREGOR SERIES~

CLAIMED BY THE HIGHLAND WOLF

TAKEN BY THE HIGHLAND WOLF

CRAVED BY THE HIGHLAND WOLF

~SILVERLAKE CITY STORIES~

HIDDEN FALLS

HUNTING CRIMSON

~STAND ALONE NOVELS~

WOLF OF MY HEART

www.ingramcontent.com/pod-product-compliance
Lightning Source LLC
Chambersburg PA
CBHW030534270626
47155CB00024B/3033